CW00517344

DEATH COMES BUT TWICE

Carlyle & West Mysteries
Book Two

David Field

SAPERE
BOOKS

DEATH COMES
BUT TWICE

Published by Sapere Books.

20 Windermere Drive, Leeds, England, LS17 7UZ,
United Kingdom

saperebooks.com

Copyright © David Field, 2020

David Field has asserted his right to be identified as the author
of this work.
All rights reserved.

No part of this publication may be reproduced, stored in any
retrieval system, or transmitted, in any form, or by any means,
electronic, mechanical, photocopying, recording, or otherwise,
without the prior written permission of the publishers.
This book is a work of fiction. Names, characters, businesses,
organisations, places and events, other than those clearly in the
public domain, are either the product of the author's
imagination, or are used fictitiously.
Any resemblances to actual persons, living or dead, events or
locales are purely coincidental.

ISBN: 978-1-80055-075-9

1

Matthew West had gratefully accepted Adelaide Carlyle's invitation to afternoon tea, in the hope that this marked a thawing of their previously somewhat frosty relationship, and in the further hope that his attraction towards her might develop into a more mutual state of affection between them.

He found her almost hypnotically appealing, as much because of her feisty temperament as her red hair, piercing green eyes and tall, slender figure, but she seemed to take great delight in holding him at arms' length.

Her father, London Hospital surgeon James Carlyle, had seemed to approve of Matthew attempting to play court to his daughter. Matthew West and James Carlyle were only recent acquaintances, thrown together when, with the additional input of Inspector John Jennings of Scotland Yard, they had investigated reports that demons from Hell had been unleashed from the bowels of the London Underground network. Matthew, a Wesleyan street preacher attached to the East End Mission in Shadwell, had been well placed, as a man of God, to assure the local populace that there were no such things as unwanted spirits returning from the dead, while Doctor Carlyle and his daughter, Adelaide, had examined the bodies of selected victims and finally worked out what was behind the visions.

It was during this brief joint enterprise that Matthew had first encountered Adelaide, who worked as her father's assistant in his mortuary in the basement of the London Hospital, and today was his first visit to their house at her invitation. He was smitten, and her father both knew it and approved of it.

Adelaide's attitude was as yet unknown and Carlyle had warned Matthew of her temperament. She was contemptuous of all men, Matthew had been advised, and she had made it her life's work to advance the cause of women in the professions. In this, she was emulating the example set by her late mother, from whom she had inherited her fire.

What Matthew had not anticipated was that Adelaide had invited two other young ladies to tea. Constance Wilberforce and Emily Peveril were Adelaide's lieutenants in the war against the male dominance of professional society, and Matthew had quickly come to realise that he had been seduced into coming here to prove his credentials. For what, precisely, remained undisclosed.

'And what is your concluded opinion regarding the position of women in your church, Mr West?' Constance Wilberforce enquired of Matthew as she leaned forward to select another cucumber sandwich in the well-appointed drawing room of the house in Victoria Park Road, Hackney.

'At present, they do not appear to be afforded one, except of course as worshippers,' Matthew hedged uncomfortably.

'And do you approve of that?' Emily Peveril asked in the manner of a police officer interrogating a suspect.

Matthew shook his head. 'Of course not. We are all God's creatures and I can find no logical justification for excluding women from the privilege of doing God's work among His people.'

'Like organising charity jumble sales and making the tea for children's Christmas parties?' Adelaide Carlyle prodded.

Matthew knew well enough to step around that one. 'If they wish to do so, then of course one would not presume to prevent that, given that they have the advantage of a greater affinity towards domestic matters. But I had more in mind the prospect that they might be allowed to preach the Gospel.'

'Under the guidance of men?' Constance asked.

'Under the guidance of one who is best placed to guide them.'

'Which at present could only be a man?' was the next verbal dart to be fired by Adelaide.

Matthew nodded. 'Of course — at present. But once women rise to positions of experience and rank within the Church, then they would be equally well placed to be the ones supplying the guidance. In the same way in which you have learned your medical skills from your own father.'

'You said "once" women rise to positions of authority,' Emily noted. 'You meant "if", surely?'

Matthew smiled. 'I was assuming that it will one day happen.'

'And you would do nothing to prevent that?' Constance demanded.

Matthew was genuinely shocked. 'Why would I? If God chooses to call someone to His work — as He once did me — then who am I to prevent that?' He was grateful for the silence that followed, if only to sip on his tea and moisten the mouth that had gone dry under the inquisition.

'You've offered to nominate Adelaide for a seat on the London County Council,' Emily cut into his thoughts. 'Do you think that having a professional man like yourself to speak for her will increase her chances of election?'

Matthew stepped deftly around this next trapdoor. Only the previous month, he had indeed agreed to nominate Adelaide for a seat on the London County Council in the elections to be held later that year. 'If Adelaide gets elected, it will be entirely on her own merits. She needed a "responsible" man to nominate her, which speaks loudly about the very wall of prejudice and inbuilt resistance that she'll be battering her head against.'

Any response this last reply might have generated was interrupted by the opening of the door from the hallway, around which the lined countenance of Dr James Carlyle peered. His short-sighted eyes sought out Matthew with a smile. 'I do apologise for the interruption, but I have an urgent need to speak with Mr West, if you could spare him from your company for a few minutes?'

It was the sort of rhetorical question that admitted of no negative answer and Matthew duly rose from his armchair with an internal sigh of relief and followed Carlyle out of the room.

Carlyle smiled knowingly from behind the desk in his study. 'I imagine that you were more than ready to be rescued from the interrogation in there.'

Matthew looked back uncertainly from his chair across the desk. 'I felt a bit like an applicant for a position in a City counting house. Those two friends of Adelaide's are almost as intimidating as she is.'

'"Faint heart never won fair lady", as the old saying goes,' Carlyle replied. 'Believe me, I've met worse in her company. Anyway, I need your urgent assistance once again.' Carlyle formed his hands into a steeple and balanced them on his waistcoated stomach. 'On Monday of this week, the body of a man calling himself Arthur Skelton was sent to me by Inspector Jennings because there were suggestions that he had been poisoned. Jennings wanted me to conduct tests and it was in fact Adelaide who managed to isolate, from his bloodstream, something called "digitalis". You probably know of it as "foxglove". It's killed many an unsuspecting peasant over the years, since the flowers look good enough to eat. It is greatly to

Adelaide's credit that she succeeded in identifying it, but Skelton's death from that cause only days before I anatomised him has given me another, and more vexing, problem.'

'You are aware that I have no medical knowledge,' Matthew replied, perplexed, 'so how do you think I may be of assistance?'

'Quite simply, in this way,' Carlyle continued. 'Unless I am gravely mistaken, this same person was hanged slightly under a year ago and you were present when that happened.'

2

'I assume you are referring to an official hanging, at Newgate?' Matthew asked after he had recovered from the initial shock of Carlyle's announcement.

Carlyle nodded. 'According to the prison records that Inspector Jennings delivered to me earlier today, the man was attended, in his final moments, by "Matthew West, of the East End Mission, Shadwell". It would seem that your clerical duties take many forms.'

Matthew grimaced. 'And that is the worst of them. Mercifully, I am rarely called upon to minister to those who are approaching death on the end of a hangman's noose, but in those cases in which the condemned man is not attended by a clergyman of his own choosing and denomination, then it has become the doleful duty of the Mission to supply one, since the regulations require it. And within the Mission I seem to be the person most regularly assigned to that grim duty. Mostly the men that I minister to have no concept of God and certainly no respect for Him. Quite apart from anything else, it's a terrible thing to hear a man cursing God in his last minutes on this earth, on his way to his own execution.'

'Quite. But what I require from you,' Carlyle told him, 'is a step by step account of what takes place during one of those awful events. I need to know how this man could have risen from the dead — unless he perfected the same trick as the man about whom you are given to preaching so ardently.'

'Only one man ever succeeded in being resurrected,' Matthew replied angrily, 'and if you require my co-operation, then it would be as well that you do not jest about that glorious event.'

'My apologies,' Carlyle murmured, 'but you should be well aware by now of my scepticism regarding matters of religion.'

'As I am suspicious of some of the actions performed in the name of medicine,' Matthew replied hotly, 'so let us agree to remain on our respective sides of those two fences, shall we?'

'Agreed,' Carlyle replied, looking for once as if he had been put in his place. 'But please oblige me by describing the process involved in hanging a man. I know that he is dropped through a trapdoor, but little else.'

Matthew's lips narrowed as he closed his eyes and recreated the scene that regularly came unbidden to his memory, often while trying to get to sleep at night. 'The condemned man is kept in a room adjoining the place where the gallows has been erected. In Newgate, regrettably, the gallows are a permanent fixture, given the number of times that they are employed. During those last few minutes I endeavour to give the man what little comfort I can, although, as I already mentioned, most of them seem to regard me as part of "the system" and rail against God with as many curses as they do the hangman.'

'Then what?' Carlyle prompted.

Matthew blanched. 'At some stage during all this the two jailors who have been in the condemned cell with us draw back the wardrobe that's been hiding the communicating door to the gallows area and knock on it from our side. The door opens and the hangman walks in and pinions the condemned man's hands behind his back with some sort of buckle. Then we form a procession, the hangman in the lead, followed by the jailors on either side of the condemned man — as often as not having to hold him upright as he screams for mercy and — ' Matthew broke off and looked away.

Carlyle nodded sagely. 'You're not the only one who respects human life and what you're telling me chills me to the bone. I can only imagine what it must be like to actually be there, but please continue — when you're able, that is.'

Matthew took several deep breaths and continued where he'd left off. 'The man is led to the trapdoor set into the floor, where his ankles are secured with another buckle. Then the prison governor, who's been waiting by the trapdoor, reads out the official order of execution and the hangman puts a hood of some sort over the head of the condemned man — and that's when I have to say the committal prayer, commending the man to the mercy of God. And I can't tell you what happens after that, since I keep my eyes closed, still praying.'

'For the soul of the condemned man?'

'For that, certainly. But also for *our* immortal souls, for the wickedness that we're committing.'

'But even if you don't watch, you must surely know what happens next?' Carlyle urged. 'That's the bit that I need to know.'

'I can only tell you what I hear. I hear the sound of a bolt being drawn back, then a kind of a rumbling sound and then a "whoosh" as the man drops through the trapdoor when it opens. By the time I open my eyes there's just an open trapdoor and a length of rope hanging tautly through the hole.'

'And afterwards?'

'The body is left hanging there for an hour or so, or so I'm told. Then the doctor goes down into the space below the trapdoor and certifies that the man's dead. "Life extinct", to use the clinically obscene title for what's just taken place.'

Carlyle looked down at the notes on his desk. 'On this occasion it was a Dr Somerskill, of whom I have no knowledge. But even a first year medical student could tell you if a man's dead or not, so I suspect that he was either bribed, or given another body entirely. What I can't understand is how the man Skelton survived the drop. He wasn't called Skelton then, by the way.'

'So how do you know it's the same man?' Matthew asked.

Carlyle consulted his fob watch. 'They should be almost finished with afternoon tea across the hallway. Much though I'm aware that you prefer my daughter's company to mine, could you indulge me for a few more minutes while I tell you something that you must keep to yourself?'

Matthew smiled grimly. 'I've either already passed or failed the examination they set me in there, so please continue.'

Carlyle sat back with a contented smile. 'There have, in recent years, been great advances in methods of identifying people. It began with a Frenchman called Alphonse Bertillion, and was further refined here in London by one of our own, Sir Francis Galton, to focus on what are called "fingerprints". Take a look at your own finger ends.'

Matthew did so, and when Carlyle asked, 'What do you see?', he screwed up his eyes and replied, 'Lots of whirly circles, with the occasional line through them, why?'

'Now examine mine,' Carlyle invited him as he extended his hand across the desk.

Matthew leaned forward and peered at them, then shrugged. 'So you've got them too — so what?'

'Do mine look like yours?'

'How can I tell? They look more or less the same, but what's your point?'

'My point is that were we both to dip our finger ends in ink, or something similar, then press them onto a piece of paper, there would be differences between them.'

'If it comes to that, we are different in height, weight, hair and eye colouring,' Matthew reminded him. 'What is the point you're trying to make?'

'We believe that no two people have the same patterns in their finger ends — "fingerprints", as they are known in the Met.'

Matthew absorbed that point for a moment. 'So you believe that people can be identified by these allegedly unique fingerprints? But there is a logical flaw in that proposal — unless you have captured and compared every single finger of every single person in the world, how can you possibly prove what you're suggesting?'

'What do you recall of what I once told you about my research methods?'

Matthew thought deeply, then shook his head. 'Sorry.'

'No need to apologise, since it was some months ago, when we were first becoming acquainted. Would it assist if I ask you to recall how I prove that the moon is not made of cream cheese?'

'I remember that, of course,' Matthew conceded, 'since I'm quite partial to cream cheese. As I recall, you prove that something doesn't exist by eliminating every logical argument that it does.'

'Excellent,' Carlyle murmured. 'So how will I prove that no two people have the same fingerprints?'

'You look for two who do,' Matthew said triumphantly. 'But my original objection is still valid — you cannot possibly examine every fingerprint in the world.'

'But if we examine all those made available to us and continue never to find two the same, does it not take us closer to the thesis that no two *are* the same?' Carlyle argued. 'At the risk of boring you, the mathematicians among us advise us that the more times that you conduct the same experiment with the same result, the more likely it is that the result in question is a universal truth.'

'Now you *have* lost me,' Matthew conceded, 'but I begin to see the light regarding this man Skelton, who was hanged under another name. You're going to tell me that the two had the same fingerprints, so they must be the same person. But how did you get the fingerprints of the dead man, and what caused you to compare them with Skelton's?'

'This is where I have to swear you to secrecy,' Carlyle replied. 'For some time now, Inspector Jennings and I have been collecting the fingerprints of everyone who comes into our respective worlds — for him it is the jail cell, while for me it is the mortuary. We already have several thousand of them and as you will have already surmised, it is our quest to find two that are the same, in the belief that we never will, thereby proving our point.

'Each of our "subjects", for want of a better word, has their finger ends dipped in a zinc solution and then impressed onto paper. We then store them in a special room at the Yard, where Jennings has a small team who compare each one that comes in with the ones they already hold. We have yet to find two the same, hence the shattering discovery that the Mr Arthur Skelton currently on my slab in the mortuary appears to be the "Artus Skuja" who was hanged on March 22nd of last year.'

'I can't say I remember the name,' Matthew admitted after a moment's thought, 'but then it's something that I try to forget. Call it the "weakness" that comes from a guilty conscience.'

'I also find capital punishment abhorrent, even though it is now conducted more humanely than in former days. The weight of the body is used to drop the victim from such a height that death is caused by what we medical men term "hyperflexion of the neck", leading to the severance of the spinal cord and the destruction of the phrenic nerve. Sorry, I see that you grow pale — should you wish to vomit, please employ the waste bin and not the carpet. But some might argue that even this brutality was too good for Skuja.'

'No-one — *ever* — deserves that!' Matthew replied angrily as he swallowed hard to suppress the gorge rising in his stomach.

Carlyle looked at him enquiringly. 'You think not? Not even though he was responsible for the deaths by burning of five innocent people while they slept?'

'Whatever he did, so called "civilised society" has no moral right to take the life of another,' Matthew insisted. 'But since you seem determined to do so, tell me why this man Skuja deserved to die.'

Carlyle searched among the papers on his desk for a small bundle that had been delivered along with the Newgate records and duly obliged. 'Artus Skuja seems to have come to England from Latvia, as part of a family of six — father, mother, two sons and two daughters — many years ago. He achieved his majority here in London and worked for many years in the Docks, where he acquired both a wiry strength and a disregard for hard, honest work. His was the classic descent into criminality, by way of petting thieving, robbery, pimping and crude forgery, until he developed a line of offending that we can only hope is unique, since it was so effective in its execution. No pun intended on that word, by the way.'

'So what did he do?' Matthew insisted.

'He managed to profit twice from the same crimes.'

'Stealing goods, then selling them back to their original owner?'

'Nothing so crude,' Carlyle told Matthew. 'To begin with it was simple arson for insurance money. He would be contacted by those whose businesses were hopelessly in debt, or unprofitable, but insured. He would be paid a substantial fee to set fire to the premises that went with those businesses, and his employer would then receive the money from the insurance company. Naturally, they would send their own investigators to examine the circumstances in which the fire had erupted, but Skuja was good at his job and not one of his clients was ever caught out in an insurance swindle. But this then suggested to him another means by which he could grow rich.'

'Working for an insurance company, to tell them how such fires might be organised?' Matthew suggested.

Carlyle shook his head. 'That would have been too honest. Instead, Skuja took to blackmailing his former customers, threatening to contact the insurance companies and advise them of how precisely the fire had been set, so as to seem a total accident.'

'Would that not also have betrayed him as the arsonist?'

'No-one ever called his bluff, and no doubt the communication with the insurance company, had one been needed, would have been anonymous.'

Matthew raised another objection. 'How did this Skuja come to be hanged? Is arson still a capital offence?'

'Not during my lifetime, as I understand it. But murder is, and that's what Skuja took the drop for. Five deaths in total.'

'An arson that went wrong?'

'Not according to the prosecuting counsel at his trial, Jennings tells me. Skuja was hired to set fire to a chemist's shop in Islington, above which was a set of rooms that the proprietor of the shop let out to a family of five — the husband and wife and their three small children. He was given

17

strict instructions by the man hiring him that he was to take whatever steps were necessary to ensure that the family were out of the place before setting light to it, but he obviously found that particular condition too irksome and simply put a match to the place late one night, while the family were sleeping. They all died, and the man who had hired him was overcome with remorse, peached on Skuja to the police, then took his own life after testifying against him.'

'A dreadful story all round,' Matthew agreed sadly. 'But you presumably already had Skuja's fingerprints on record when the body of this man calling himself Skelton was delivered to you?'

'Yes indeed, but along with the corpse and fingerprints, I received the depressing news that our experiment had failed, since the finger impressions taken from the corpse when it was removed from the house that Skelton was then living in, discovered by his landlord, had already been subjected to the process and some eagle-eyed member of Jennings's team had spotted the similarity. Believe me, five separate people have since conducted the same minute comparison process and there can be no doubt. Either Skuja and Skelton are one and the same, or two years of painstaking work goes up in smoke.'

'Hardly an appropriate turn of phrase, in the circumstances,' Matthew said. 'But I'd take an intelligent guess that your greatest interest is in preserving your experiment. This requires that somehow you prove that Skuja and Skelton are the same person. Hence your request for me to become involved, since I was there when it happened. But since I have no recollection of one among a dozen or so of those dreadful events, how may I even begin to help?'

Carlyle consulted his notes before looking back up at Matthew with a smile. 'Does it assist your memory if I advise you that Skuja was one of three men executed that morning? They must have had a pressing queue or something.'

Matthew shook his head. 'I've never been present at more than one execution in a single day and I doubt if I could have withstood such an ordeal. Even if I could, I can assure you that I'd remember it.'

'They weren't all dropped at the same time,' Carlyle told him as he continued to study the notes. 'Skuja was the second of the day, at 9 am, with a man called Jack Riddings dispatched an hour earlier and finally Joshua Zammit at ten o'clock. There is an interesting additional fact surrounding the three deaths, however. The first is that the same doctor certified all three deaths. His name is Albert Somerskill, and he has a general practice in Limehouse, which can hardly be the most lucrative of places to set up shop, so he may be open to a little bribery. If there's some drug that can simulate death, I'd like to know about it.'

'Do you have any theory of your own as to how it might have been done — assuming, that is, that Skuja *did* escape the hangman?' Matthew asked.

Carlyle tapped his teeth thoughtfully before replying. 'You're probably aware of this anyway, but the length of the rope in modern hangings is carefully calculated so as to ensure that the neck is firmly broken. The lighter the condemned man, the longer the drop. The prison records show that Skuja was allocated a rope that would play out for some six feet prior to the final jerk that would end his life, so that he would be out of sight of everyone standing by the hatch — even those who, unlike you, did not have their eyes closed.'

'And from this you surmise what?' Matthew asked.

'Skuja didn't actually reach that final jerk,' Carlyle explained. 'There was a mattress, or something like that, waiting to catch him below the line of the hatch.'

Matthew thought that through for a moment, then raised the obvious objection. 'If that were the case, then those who had their eyes open — not to mention those whose dreadful duty it was to cut down the body after an hour or so — *and* the attending physician — would have seen that happen, or at least be aware that it had. They would need to have been bribed. All of them, including the executioner himself.'

Carlyle smiled. 'Now you begin to appreciate the enormity of the problem that confronts you.'

'I haven't agreed to get involved.'

'No,' Carlyle said, 'but you are about to. That's assuming, of course, that you wish to continue playing court to Adelaide.'

'I'm nowhere near "playing court" to her yet, more's the pity,' Matthew objected. 'I don't even know if I've passed the rigorous test of being allowed to nominate her for the LCC elections later this year. But if you're going to withdraw my privilege of meeting with her if I refuse, then of course I must do as you ask.'

'I think you may have misinterpreted what I said a moment ago,' Carlyle said. 'I would never seek to interfere with any ambition on your part to worm your way into Adelaide's affections, but if you are to work closely with Jennings and myself in the matter of Skelton's seeming resurrection, then you will have greater excuse to be visiting both the mortuary and this house.'

'There's that, I suppose,' Matthew conceded, 'but where do I start?'

'I would dearly love to know if the level below the hatch in the gallows area would admit of something such as a mattress,'

Carlyle told him. 'Then I need to know just how reliable are the witnesses to Skuja's alleged execution. The attendant physician, as I already mentioned, was a Dr Albert Somerskill. The two jailors assisting the hangman were Sam Tibbins and John Tasker, according to what's written here. Then there's the hangman himself.'

'I know James Billington from the previous occasions when I've attended executions,' Matthew confirmed.

Carlyle nodded. 'Which makes it all the more suspicious that his was not the hand on the trapdoor on this occasion. Seemingly he was indisposed and his place was taken by one of his apprentices — a man called Percy Bryant.'

Matthew's eyes glazed over slightly as he stared into the middle distance and the memory came back to him. '*Now* I remember — or at least, I think I do. There was a time when James wasn't there and one of the jailers joked about him having had a bad oyster the night before. The man who was replacing him didn't seem all that amused and ordered the jailor to keep his remarks to himself and see to his duties.'

'See, it's all coming back to you,' Carlyle pointed out reassuringly, just as the door from the hall opened and Adelaide's face appeared round it.

'Emily and Constance have just left,' she told them, 'so I'll be in my room if I'm required for anything before supper. Will Matthew be staying on to take supper with us?'

'Did I pass the examination?' Matthew asked cheekily.

Adelaide allowed herself a weak smile. 'I'm not sure to what "examination" you're referring, but Emily and Constance have no objection to you being my first nominator. There's still the matter of a second one. Have you got around to asking your brother yet?'

'I did, but he insists on meeting you first.'

'Only appropriate. Invite him to take afternoon tea with us one day next week — we still have nearly two weeks before the nominations have to be in.'

'If it's all the same to you,' Matthew replied, 'we might combine that with something he requires of me, which is to cast my eye over his latest lady friend and advise him whether or not she's worthy of one day inheriting his portion of the family fortune. He seems quite set on her and of course I'd value your opinion as well, so it might be best if you call upon us. It's a modest enough house by your standards, but my mother would deem it an honour to have the daughter of a London Hospital surgeon taking tea in our sitting room.'

'Consider it done, then. Just let me know which day.'

'Won't your father need to approve your taking time off from your mortuary duties?'

'He'll agree, won't you, Father?'

She closed the door behind her and Carlyle grinned. 'You see? You even need to remain in my good books in order to be able to take Adelaide home to meet your family.'

3

Matthew watched with a smile as the handful or so who had attended his Bible class in the East End Mission left the room after his final blessing and made their way down the hallway to the free dinner that, if he was to be honest with himself, was what had really brought them in. He had no false pride regarding his abilities as a bringer of God's good word, but something about this morning's class had tweaked his conscience.

The theme for today had been 'Christ's ministry among the heathen' and inevitably it had turned his thoughts back to those awful memories of men who had committed such heinous crimes — usually against their fellow man — that society had condemned them to end their lives prematurely. True evangelism was not conducted among the wealthy and comfortably placed in society, he reminded himself, but those who had fallen to the lowest level. His great hero, John Wesley, had not set up his table inside the finely appointed Georgian squares of Whitehall and Piccadilly, but had sought out the working-class slums, the docks, the mills and the shipyards to preach that all men are equal under God.

There was surely more grace to be earned by following in the footsteps of those who had shown the way in ministering to the lowly than there was by feasting in the halls of the wealthy. That was what had drawn Matthew to the Wesleyan Church in the first place and he should be ashamed of himself for shrinking from the Lord's true work when it came to offering comfort to those about to be hanged.

His thoughts drifted back to the promise he'd given to Carlyle only the previous afternoon. Then came the realisation that he was by no means the only clergyman who was called upon to attend hangings. He was in reality not called upon very often and yet the prison regulations required the presence of a 'chaplain' at every execution.

Carlyle had advised him that the man Skuja had been one of three executed that morning. This in itself was unusual, in Matthew's limited experience, but it clearly meant that at least one other clergyman would have been in attendance for the other two. Matthew knew from his own experience that everyone entering Newgate was required to sign in a visitors' book. It would be a simple matter to look in that book and identify who the other attending clergymen had been.

An hour later, Matthew shivered as usual as the heavy prison gate clanged shut behind him. He was aware of the suspicious eyes of the gatekeeper watching to ensure that he really was heading for the administration office. His current lowly status within the Wesleyan Church, without any attachment to a particular 'living', meant that he was not authorised to wear the standard 'dog collar' by which the clergy were normally readily identifiable, but his face was just about familiar enough to those who guarded London's oldest working prison for him to be grudgingly admitted.

It was the same inside the administration office, where a stony-faced clerk pushed the visitors' book across the counter towards him.

'I'm seeking to locate another clergyman who was here on a day last year,' Matthew explained, then silently asked God for forgiveness as he launched into what he hoped was only a little white lie. 'We got talking and I promised to look him up, but unfortunately I lost the piece of paper on which I'd written down his particulars.'

'You one o' them church types?' the clerk asked.

When Matthew confirmed that he was, the clerk reached for another volume on the shelf to the side of him and handed it to Matthew with a gruff, 'It'd be one o' them 'angin' days, then. We 'as a separate book for them what's due ter be 'ung. Yer musta signed it yerself, if yer really are who yer sez yer are,' he added suspiciously.

Matthew flicked back the pages until he came to the entries for March 22nd of the previous year. Sure enough, there was his own signature and alongside that was the name of the condemned man, Artus Skuja. In the row above that was the name 'Thomas Enderby', who had apparently been ministering to both Jack Riddings, due for the drop at 8am and Joshua Zammit, at ten am.

Matthew looked back across at the clerk. 'Might I please have a piece of paper and pen?' he asked. 'I need to make a note of this name.'

'If that's why yer come 'ere in the first place,' the clerk asked, his suspicions now thoroughly aroused, 'why didn't yer bring some paper've yer own?'

Matthew had no answer to that other than a pale apologetic smile and some excuse about being 'the world's biggest bumblebrain', but the clerk was by no means convinced and he pulled a lever just below the counter. Matthew heard a clunking sound as the door to the office locked automatically.

'Just ter make sure yer are who yer sez yer is,' the clerk told him, 'tell me who yer know inside 'ere who can vouch fer yer.'

Matthew thought hard and remembered a name. 'John Tasker,' he told the clerk with a far from confident smile. 'He works in the Condemned Wing.'

The clerk turned to a younger man seated behind him in the office and instructed him to go in search of John Tasker, then he turned back to Matthew with a piece of paper he ripped from a pile at his elbow. 'There's the paper yer was wantin', but till Tasker gets 'ere an' vouches fer yer, yer'll not be leavin', so yer may as well take yer time about it.'

With nothing better to do, and having noted the name of the clergyman who he would need to locate if he ever got out of this terrible place, Matthew occupied his time idling through the visitors' book lying open in front of him. He knew that condemned men were allowed visitors, unlike other prisoners, and curiosity coaxed him into searching the entries for the days and weeks prior to Skuja's execution to see if anyone had cared for him enough to visit.

On the day before his execution, Skuja had been visited by a woman called Bridget Dempsey. A quick flick back through the understandably uncluttered pages of this grim record also revealed that this same woman, and no-one else, had been a regular visitor since three days after Skuja's committal to Newgate. In all, this Bridget Dempsey had made four visits, each several days apart from the others and she was obviously worth talking to, if Matthew could ever locate her. The name sounded Irish, and perhaps Inspector Jennings might be willing to assist, on the pretext that she might be a secret Fenian agent.

The outside door creaked open and the florid double-chinned smile of John Tasker appeared. 'Yeah, this is the Rev'rend West, from the East End Mission,' he confirmed. 'Seems like yer aroused the admission clerk's suspicions, my friend,' he said as he turned his attention to Matthew, then looked down at the book on the counter in front of him and asked, 'What yer lookin' at that fer?'

'I was checking up on a name for that day when you did three hangings in a row,' Matthew told him. 'I needed to know who the other clergymen were that day, but as it turned out there was only one more, who ministered to both of the other two.'

'And who were that?' Tasker asked.

Matthew pointed down at the paper on which he'd written the name 'Rev. Thomas Enderby'.

Tasker appeared to check himself momentarily as he also read the woman's name that Matthew had written below it. 'Why d'yer need to speak to 'er?' Tasker asked, almost accusingly.

Matthew was immediately on the defensive. 'I don't, really. I was intrigued to learn that a miserable excuse for a human being like Skuja received a visitor and I suppose that curiosity got the better of me.'

'She were a right doxie,' Tasker told him. 'I reckon yer could catch a nasty disease just talkin' to 'er, so I'd keep me distance if I was you.'

'I'll bear that in mind — thanks,' Matthew said as he picked up the paper, handed the pen back over the counter and walked outside.

Now he had two — and possibly three — people he needed to speak to. The first was a Dr Albert Somerskill, with a practice somewhere in Limehouse, who should be easy enough to trace. The second, a clergyman called Thomas Enderby, who was most likely an Anglican from a nearby parish, assuming that the two condemned men to whom he had been ministering had been East End men. And, if God sought to smile upon him, perhaps also an Irish-born prostitute called Bridget Dempsey.

4

Matthew smiled to himself as he hurried down the stairs to the basement level inside the London Hospital; very few people, he imagined, would be eager to visit a hospital mortuary, but he had two pleasant reasons for doing so. The first was to report progress to Carlyle, and the second was to confirm with his beautiful daughter that she would be available to take afternoon tea in Clerkenwell in two afternoons' time.

'I hope that I may be forgiven for not awaiting an invitation to enter,' he breezed as he stepped inside after the briefest of knocks, 'but I have two important pieces of information.'

Carlyle nodded over the top of the cadaver that was laid out, face down, on the slab in front of him, then tactfully covered it over with the sheet that had previously been lowered to knee level. 'Do come in, Matthew. We're probably due a cup of tea and this gentleman can wait. Adelaide, would you do the honours, please? Matthew will no doubt be in need of a cup when he learns the identity of the man under this sheet.'

'Not another manifestation of the resurrected Artus Skuja?' Matthew joked lightly as he looked away from the slab. He realised that he was not the only visitor when a stern voice from the corner of the room announced, 'If you were looking for Doctor Somerskill, you've found him.'

Matthew shook hands with Inspector John Jennings and said, 'He was to be the next person on my list. What's he doing here?'

'This is where Inspector Jennings brings a good number of his recently deceased,' Adelaide commented as she turned back from lighting the gas burner under the large water flask and emptied tea leaves into the adjacent teapot.

'He was found at the top of an alleyway a few streets away from where he'd been called to visit a sick patient,' Jennings explained. 'According to what we learned from his wife the address he was given was that of a new patient. Needless to say the address is non-existent.'

'So he was lured out on a false pretence?' Matthew asked. 'And then murdered, I assume, since he's here on the slab?'

'Correct,' Carlyle confirmed, 'although on this occasion Scotland Yard hardly required my services.' He lowered the sheet again and Matthew gasped slightly as he saw the depth to which the wicked looking knife was embedded in the back of the deceased.

'The first conclusion drawn by the local plod was that it was a simple robbery, since his medical bag was missing,' Jennings explained. 'But then they were tipped off by a local pawnbroker that two street urchins had attempted to pawn some very specialist medical tools, and when they were held up against a wall and threatened with the immediate application of two billy clubs they advised us that they'd come across the victim face down while sizing up the possibility of breaking into the cobbler's workshop at the top of the alley. They apparently grabbed the medical bag and ran when they saw the blood and the knife in his back.'

'When was this, and how come the Yard's been called in for a routine murder?' Matthew asked.

Jennings sighed. 'It's a sad reflection on life in this part of London when you can describe the knifing of a local doctor as a "routine murder", but you're right of course. I wasn't called in as such, but all serious crimes anywhere in Her Majesty's capital city are wired in to the Yard under standing regulations and I recognised the name. I immediately sent a wire back to Limehouse and had the body brought here. I got here a few minutes before you did and since you knew nothing about the death of Dr Somerskill two nights ago, I assume that you have some other reason to be here?'

'Two reasons, actually,' Matthew explained. 'So far as Dr Somerskill's concerned, I can't help you, but I've identified the clergyman who attended the other two hangings on the morning that Skuja was hanged. He dealt with both of them and I believe that he may have been an Anglican, although I don't yet know which parish.'

'So the same man acted as chaplain for both the hanging before Skuja's and then the one afterwards?' Carlyle queried, and when Matthew nodded, he asked, 'Doesn't that strike you as a little unusual? Why didn't they conduct his two one after the other, leaving yours until last?'

'I've been wondering about that,' Matthew replied. 'Could it be that there's something significant in Skuja taking the drop in between two others? Something that was important in the subterfuge surrounding his death?'

'Even more significant,' Carlyle said as he looked down at the body on the slab, 'is how an experienced doctor was fooled into certifying Skuja's death.'

'I'm working on the theory that he was bribed and then done to death on the order of whoever bribed him,' Jennings told them.

Carlyle raised both eyebrows. 'Are you suggesting that a member of my profession stooped to criminal deception?'

'It's one explanation,' Jennings replied with one of his trademark smirks. 'And before you get on your high horse about the integrity of your profession, do you know how many illegal abortions we have to deal with every year in the Met?'

'At least they're done professionally in those cases,' Adelaide observed with a snort. 'Better than some of those dreadful bungled jobs in seedy parlours up back streets. If our *male* politicians would only take an interest in the crying need for some sort of birth control method being legalised, then hundreds of women a year would not be driven to those appalling extremities.'

'You sound like a seasoned politician already,' Matthew said. 'And that was my second reason for coming here this afternoon. If you can make yourself available on Thursday afternoon, you're invited to tea.'

'Not before time,' Adelaide replied.

Jennings moved the conversation on. 'So what else have you discovered, if anything, young man?'

Matthew told them of the several visits to Skuja by a woman calling herself Bridget Dempsey.

Jennings's eyes opened wide. 'That gives me every excuse to continue investigating this whole weird business. With a name like that she's bound to be a Fenian, and the Yard has an entire Division looking into their activities. If I can demonstrate a link between those and Skuja, I can bring other men into the enquiry.'

'According to one of the jailers who met her, she's little better than a prostitute,' Matthew told him, to another snort from Adelaide.

'Typical male conclusion. Any woman not accompanied by a man *must* be on the game. For all we know she was his wife, or lady friend, or something along those lines. She probably adopted an assumed name rather than expose herself to the public disgrace of being associated with a murderer.'

'No-one claimed Skuja's body,' Carlyle reminded her.

'Have you any idea how much it costs to have a person buried these days?' Adelaide countered.

'What *did* happen to it?' Matthew asked.

'It was buried where it belonged,' Jennings replied, 'in the pit inside Newgate where all those hanged are laid to rest, with a bucketful of lime on top of them, to hasten their disappearance.'

'You persuaded the prison authorities that he was really Skuja and not "Skelton"?' Matthew asked.

Jennings nodded. 'It was either that or a full-scale public enquiry, based on the evidence of the identical fingerprints. The governor was most co-operative.'

'Which is more than can be said of the staff in the administration office when I searched the visitor records on the pretence of learning who had been ministering to the other two men hanged that day,' Matthew muttered.

'What did you expect?' Jennings replied. 'If there was a mistake at the hanging, they'd be under firm instructions to cover it up. But that also makes Matthew a target, does it not?'

'Not before he signs my nomination paper, I hope,' Adelaide quipped, and Matthew was relieved to note that she was smiling kindly at him.

'Does that mean that you want me to leave things alone?' Matthew asked of Carlyle, who shook his head.

'Not if you have the courage to continue, my boy.'

'I probably have the courage,' Matthew confirmed, 'but I'm still missing several important facts.'

'Such as?' Jennings asked.

'Such as what the resurrected Skuja was up to, in his new identity as Arthur Skelton, to entice someone to poison him. We *are* assuming that he was murdered, are we not?'

'We are,' Jennings confirmed, 'but given the somewhat unusual circumstances of his second death, we're back-peddling a little on the investigation. It's not as if we had a family, or anyone else, demanding answers. As to your original question, there have been several suspicious fires in and around the East End in recent months, so my first thought was that he'd been back to his old tricks. But when I made enquiries with the insurance companies involved, none of them could come up with any suggestion that the fires had been deliberately set. So perhaps he'd retired.'

'You're forgetting the other arm of his criminal enterprise,' Carlyle reminded them both. 'Perhaps he was blackmailing people — that would give someone a very powerful motive to do away with him.'

'Perhaps he committed suicide?' Matthew suggested, to a ribald snort from both Carlyle and Adelaide at the same time.

'You need a certain basic botanical knowledge to convert foxglove into digitalis,' Carlyle told him. 'We have no reason to believe, from Skuja's previous life history, that he had any such background, and in any case, had he simply wanted to kill himself, then a knife to the wrists would be just as effective. Or a gun to the head. And why would he commit suicide within a year of having gone to great lengths to preserve himself from the noose?'

'So who else might have wanted him dead?' Matthew asked.

'Whoever he was currently blackmailing,' Jennings suggested. 'Perhaps even someone who'd been involved in his escape from the hangman.'

Matthew grinned. 'Even I can pick the flaw in that. How could he threaten to expose someone who'd been behind his escape without revealing to the world who he really was and being sent back into Newgate for the job to be done properly the second time?'

'A valid point,' Jennings conceded. 'So where will you investigate next? Do you require my assistance?'

'If I do, I'll let you know,' Matthew assured him. 'But I hardly think I'll need protection from the Reverend Thomas Enderby, assuming that I can locate him.'

'And assuming that he exists,' Carlyle reminded him. 'Now let's have some of that tea, shall we?'

5

Matthew took a deep breath before walking smartly into the sitting room, where his younger brother Charles leaped to his feet with a broad smile and indicated the fair-haired young lady seated next to him on the sofa. 'Here he comes at last,' Charles announced. 'My big brother Matthew, late as usual. Matthew, please let me introduce you to Miss Susan Byfield.'

'Delighted, I'm sure,' Matthew murmured as he leaned down to take the offered hand, which was slightly cool and damp. He took the seat nearest to the window, from which he could keep an eye out for Adelaide's coach arriving.

'Charles tells me that you're a clergyman,' Susan said in order to fill the ensuing awkward silence.

Matthew inclined his head in a gesture of confirmation. 'Yes and no. I am indeed ordained, but I await an appointment to a church of my own.'

'Before you enquire how a clergyman can exist without a church,' Charles intervened hastily, 'let me explain that the Church movement to which Matthew belongs is a fairly informal one by contemporary standards, and its ministers are engaged in all sorts of charity work among the poor. Matthew is attached to the East End Mission down in Shadwell.'

'Our parents were very religious — and my mother still is — so we attended church regularly every Sunday,' Susan said. 'Not anymore, though.'

'We?' Matthew asked, if only to keep the conversation going.

Susan nodded. 'I have a stepsister. Or perhaps "had" might be more accurate, since I haven't kept up with her regularly since our father died. He left us all very well provided for, and while I used my share of the legacy to keep on the greengrocery business that he'd built up, Mary — my stepsister — took herself off to Sussex, and apart from the occasional letter I've no idea how she's getting on. She could be dead for all I know, although she's only a few years older than me.'

'Susan owns that massive greengrocery alongside Farringdon Market,' Charles enthused. 'We met when I was helping Toby Parsons choose the buttonhole flowers for the groomsmen at his wedding. I went back a few times, pretending to be interested in buying vegetables for Mother's excellent soups, and managed to engage her attention sufficiently that she very charitably agreed to walk out with me a few times — and here we are.'

Matthew heard the unmistakable sound of iron wheels grinding to a halt under the window and looked down. Adelaide was about to descend from her coach through the door that Collins was holding open and Matthew leapt to his feet. 'Here comes Adelaide — Miss Carlyle — I'll just go down and welcome her.'

Matthew rushed down the stairs that led from the apartments occupied by the West family above the family business. He greeted Adelaide and escorted her back up to the sitting room.

Charles rose politely to his feet as Matthew said, 'Miss Adelaide Carlyle. Please meet my brother Charles and his lady friend Miss Susan Byfield.'

No sooner had Adelaide taken the seat on the other side of the sofa from the one occupied by Matthew than Matthew's parents entered — his mother carrying a large cake, followed behind by his father, bearing plates, cutlery and napkins. Matthew effected the introductions to his parents and Alice West smiled down at Adelaide as she laid the cake on the table.

'Matthew insisted that I make one of my strawberry jam cakes, so I hope that you find this one to your taste.'

'I'm sure I will,' Adelaide replied with a gracious smile, then looked beyond Alice West as another figure appeared in the doorway, carefully balancing a tray of tea things, but with a large sketchbook clutched ominously under her arm.

'My sister Caroline,' Matthew said.

'I've seen some of your work. You're a very talented artist,' Adelaide said.

'Charles tells me that you're intending to stand for a seat on the LCC,' Susan chimed in. 'That's frightfully brave of you, since it consists entirely of men.'

'That won't always be the case, if I get my way,' Adelaide smiled defiantly.

'But you need two men to nominate you, do you not?' Charles asked. 'Matthew has already agreed, as I understand it, and you're hoping that I will also. But before I do that, I'd be grateful if you'd disclose what your plans are, should you succeed. Apart from putting men in their places, that is.'

Adelaide preened herself and nodded her approval as Matthew gestured towards the tea pot. While he poured her a cup of tea, adding a slice of lemon that he'd gone to the trouble of bringing in earlier that day, since he knew that she preferred her tea like that, served black, Adelaide began to answer Charles's question.

'Housing, for a start. It's little wonder that there's so much crime in the poorer parts of London when people are required to live in such hovels. The LCC has begun a programme of rehousing in the worst slum areas, but to my mind it's only a combination of token gestures and an opportunity for their friends to get fat and wealthy from the contracts that will be handed out. Then there are the streets, which are a health hazard all by themselves — all that horse manure, which ought to be removed by swifter and more mechanical means. As for the river — well, would *you* bathe in it?'

'I think I've heard enough already to persuade me to vote for you,' Susan said appreciatively.

'Do you qualify to vote, my dear?' Adelaide asked.

'I most certainly do,' Susan announced proudly. 'I'm a business owner in my own name.'

'Susan has the largest greengrocery business east of Holborn,' Charles told Adelaide, who nodded.

'You should regard that vote as a privilege, although the fact that it qualifies as such is another disgrace that I intend to work towards eliminating. The employment of property qualifications as a basis for suffrage automatically eliminates most women from the voting process for the LCC, and even I only qualify because my father generously put our Hackney house in my name once I came of age. In order to qualify to nominate for a seat on the LCC one needs to be eligible to vote in the elections, so the powers that be keep women down twice by the same simple action.'

While this conversation had been going on, Caroline had been seated on the arm of the sofa, staring intently at Adelaide and occasionally drawing swift and confident pencil lines on a blank page in her sketchpad. She rose and slid from the room, leaving the sketchpad propped up against the side of the sofa. Charles reached down, picked it up, whistled softly and showed it in turn to Adelaide and Matthew.

'What a talent!' Adelaide said admiringly. She turned to Caroline as she re-entered the room. 'Caroline, when you've finished this excellent likeness of me, could I please take it home to show to my father? He's always on at me to get my portrait painted, like my mother once did, since he wants to hang the two alongside each other in our sitting room. It smacks too much of vanity to me, but this might serve to satisfy his requirement and perhaps buy me some peace.'

'Actually,' Caroline replied awkwardly, 'I was hoping that you might use it in your campaign for a seat on the LCC. Every candidate has their picture on posters and things, don't they, and on the little leaflet things that they hand out to voters?'

'They do indeed,' Adelaide confirmed, 'but I was thinking of going to one of those professional photographers.'

'Take my advice and don't,' Charles butted in. 'Speaking as a professional printer I can tell you that it's much harder to cut a half tone block from a photograph than it is a pen and ink drawing, which is why the daily papers still employ artists like Caroline hopes to be. We could turn out hundreds, if not thousands, of the sort of thing you have in mind, at half the cost, if you use Caroline's sketch. I'm sure we could also do you a *very* reasonable price.'

'And if I give you and your father the business, you'll nominate me?' Adelaide asked with a coquettish smile. 'After all, you'd be losing out on a business proposition if you didn't agree.'

'I'd already decided to do that,' Charles said with a smile.

6

The following morning, Matthew presented himself at the cottage that went with the curacy of St Dunstan's Parish Church, Stepney and asked to speak to the Reverend Thomas Enderby. The lady who answered the door looked a little askance when Matthew told her that he was a clergyman himself but seemed reasonably satisfied with the explanation that his dog collar was currently at the laundry.

'They *are* very difficult to keep clean, as I should know,' she said, 'but tell your wife to soak them first in a solution of half vinegar and half water.'

Thanking her for her advice, Matthew was ushered into a cramped back room of the type that would probably become familiar to him if he ever got a living of his own.

Thomas Enderby rose from behind a pile of paper on his desk and extended an ink-stained hand in greeting. 'My wife tells me that you're from the East End Mission,' he said. 'I hope that you're not recruiting — I've done my bit for the poor and needy. Now I minister to the wealthy and self-satisfied. Would you care for a pre-prandial sherry, since it's almost time for dinner, or "luncheon", as I must learn to call it if I'm to be socially acceptable to a depressing proportion of my parishioners? However, since I'm only the curate around here, I can leave the pretentiousness to the vicar and get on with preserving souls.'

The man was obviously fond of his own voice and Matthew was hopeful of making use of that in a moment or two, but in the meantime he graciously declined the offer of a sherry on the ground that it was contrary to the teachings of his Church.

Enderby smiled. 'Yes, of course. You're one of those Wesleyan types, aren't you? I should have remembered that they run the Mission in Shadwell. So what brings you here? Presumably not lessons in theology from the High Church?'

'No.' Matthew allowed himself to smile. 'I'm here to enquire about a double hanging at which you were the chaplain. Newgate, March of last year. Jack Riddings and Joshua Zammit?'

Enderby's smile faded slightly. 'The two ex-soldiers who murdered a man they were robbing down in Smithfield?'

'I've no idea what crimes had led to their hangings,' Matthew explained. 'My interest is in the fact that they met God on either side of a soul for whom I was responsible.'

'A triple hanging, you mean? I don't remember that.'

'No, forgive me, I didn't express myself very well,' Matthew replied, as he referred to the notes he had made under the eagle eye of the visitors' office clerk in Newgate. 'Jack Riddings was despatched at 8 am and Joshua Zammit at 10 am. The hanging in between — at 9 am — was one of mine. A man called "Artus Skuja".'

'They were a tragic pair,' Enderby began to reminisce as he gazed into the middle distance. 'Former Grenadier Guards who fell on hard times after they were thrown out for brawling in the Mess. I was, in a former life, an Army padre, you see, and from time to time I came across them in the soup kitchen that my wife runs every Saturday in the churchyard across the road. Some ex-Army men never adapt properly to civilian life, and those two couldn't take to manual labour, so they sank further and further down the poverty scale. Then they committed the crime for which they were sentenced to death and they asked if I'd be there when they were executed. A dreadful business altogether. What's your opinion of the death penalty?'

'I'm vehemently opposed to it,' Matthew replied.

Enderby nodded. 'It's so "clinical" and impersonal, isn't it? Not to mention brutal.'

'It's more humane than it used to be, or so I'm informed,' Matthew told him. 'Was this one your first?'

Enderby nodded. 'First — and second, of course. Hopefully there won't be a third. I imagine that you have to attend them regularly, given that you minister to less law-abiding types than I do.'

'Far too regularly,' Matthew agreed. 'But since they were the only ones that you've ever seen go out of this life on the end of a hangman's rope, do you remember anything unusual about that occasion?'

'Not really,' Enderby admitted. 'The first was a bit of a shock to the system. *My* system, I mean, although it was obviously a bit of a rude experience for poor old Jack Riddings as well. He was awarded a bravery medal in the Sudan, did you know that?'

'I knew nothing about either of them,' Matthew admitted. 'My man was sandwiched in between your two, time-wise. So you had to wait for quite a long while in that dreadful tea-room for the second one to take the drop?'

'No, as it turns out,' Enderby replied. 'It's coming back to me now. There must have been some reason why your chappie went early, because I was called back up to that awful gallows room just after half-past nine and told that Zammitt's death had been brought forward. Saved him another half hour of mental agony, I suppose, although he probably didn't deserve it. He was the worse of the two, in my experience and I wouldn't be surprised to learn that he was the one who led poor old Jack Riddings astray.'

'So your second man — this "Zammit" — was executed shortly after nine-thirty?' Matthew asked as calmly as he could, although the hairs on the back of his neck were alerting him to something important.

'Yes, like I said. I wasn't complaining, obviously, since it meant that I got out of that dreadful place a bit earlier. I don't suppose Zammit was in any position to protest, either, in the circumstances.'

'Would you be surprised to learn that according to the jail records Zammit's execution took place at 10 am?'

'Not really. Bureaucracy and all that. Why — is it important?'

Matthew was tempted to reply that it could be crucial to an investigation he was conducting, but restricted himself to thanking Enderby profusely for his assistance, politely refusing a second offer of sherry and making his way back outside.

'Don't forget to tell your wife about that trick with the dog collars,' Mrs Enderby reminded him as she showed him out with a sherry decanter and two glasses on a tray in her hands.

'I'm not married,' Matthew told her and hid his blushes as she replied quietly, 'What a waste.'

During his deliberately long walk back down Stepney High Street on his return to the Mission, Matthew was thinking hard, but getting nowhere. He was convinced that there was some significance in the fact that an indecent period of haste had separated the alleged execution of Skuja and the hanging of Zammit. If he could work out why, he was part way towards being able to report progress to Carlyle, which would give him another excuse to call in at the London Hospital.

'Here's the first galley pull of your lady friend's election poster,' Charles told Matthew as he slipped the single sheet down on the supper table alongside his plate of pork chops, then took his seat next to their sister Caroline on the other side of the table.

'I don't suppose there's any point in advising you *yet again* that she's not my lady friend?' Matthew muttered as he cast his eye over what had been produced in the printing shop one floor below them. They had done more than justice to Caroline's fine portrait of Adelaide, and Matthew was aware of his sister's eyes across the table, searching his face for his first response. He smiled across at her. 'You've caught her likeness very well.'

'It was easy, since she has such elegant bone structure,' Caroline replied.

'Little wonder that Matthew's so taken with her,' Charles goaded, earning the anticipated response that 'I'm *not* "taken with her", as you put it.'

'Yes you are,' Caroline chimed in as she helped herself to roast potatoes from the dish in the centre of the table. 'Sorry, Matthew, but you don't hide it very well.'

'A bit out of your league, all the same,' Charles continued relentlessly. 'A big house in her own name and Daddy a fancy surgeon and all that. Why would she be interested in a humble preacher?'

'She's not interested in marriage,' Matthew replied.

'How do you know that?' Charles asked. 'Have you asked her?'

'I don't have to,' Matthew grumbled. 'She makes it very obvious from time to time. It seems to be her mission in life to prove that women can exist in society without men.'

'Not if they want children, they can't,' his mother observed.

Caroline grimaced. 'I don't think I'd be interested in that horrible process.'

'You're only eighteen years old,' her father added as he finished his second chop and wiped his mouth on his napkin. 'Time enough for that when you're well over twenty-one. And while you're all badgering Matthew about his love life, no-one's making any comment about the poster.'

Matthew looked more closely at what Charles had placed next to his supper plate and read the few brief lines in bold capital letters.

HELP ME CLEAN UP LONDON!
A VOTE FOR ME MEANS:
1. CLEANER STREETS
2. A HEALTHIER RIVER
3. BETTER HOUSING FOR WORKERS
AT THE LCC ELECTIONS, MAKE THIS HAPPEN
— VOTE FOR ADELAIDE CARLYLE — HACKNEY
WARD.

'We made up the wording from what she told us when she came for tea,' Charles explained. 'What did she think of Susan, by the way?'

'I haven't seen her since,' Matthew replied.

'Well you'll need to get her approval for that poster,' George West told him. 'We've got the run-off slotted in for next Monday, so we need to know by then.'

7

Matthew awoke the following morning with the pleasant thought that he had an excuse to visit Adelaide and her father in the London Hospital, then sighed when he also recalled that Superintendent Livingstone had been in touch asking him to arrive on time at the Mission to meet someone regarding the current laws surrounding the death penalty. He checked himself with the thought that he was here on this earth to minister to others and to ensure that God's love was bestowed on all His people. *All* of them, not just beautiful ones who'd captured his interest and who were probably beyond his reach anyway, as Charles had cruelly reminded him the previous evening.

So with a still nagging reluctance he took the horse bus down Farringdon Road and presented himself at the superintendent's office just as St Paul's was chiming out nine o'clock of the forenoon. There was someone in there already and as Matthew appeared in the doorway the superintendent waved him in, then gestured towards his visitor.

'Matthew, allow me to introduce Mrs Miller.'

'Please call me Mary, if we're to be working together,' she invited, as she rose to her feet and held out her gloved hand for Matthew to shake. She was tall and elegantly dressed in a deep mauve two piece with matching bonnet and gloves, while the perfume in which she was modestly doused was redolent of a West End speciality house.

Matthew looked back enquiringly towards the superintendent, who smiled. 'I took the liberty of advising Mrs Miller, when she enquired after you, that of all those attached to the Mission you were indeed the most likely to be sympathetic to her cause.'

'I wish to see capital punishment abolished for ever from this nation,' she explained with a winning smile. 'It's a blot upon our Christian way of life and an abomination in the sight of the Lord. Also an obscenity in its method of achievement.'

'I wouldn't disagree with any of that,' Matthew replied, a little puzzled. 'But from what the superintendent just said, I gather that you were seeking me out particularly. I'm by no means the only Mission minister who thinks as we do, so why me?'

'You were recommended by someone inside Newgate,' she replied enigmatically and Matthew was about to enquire who, when Superintendent Livingstone gave a polite cough and told Matthew, 'I've left word that your usual consultation room be made available for you and Mrs Miller.'

Taking the hint, Matthew escorted the lady down the hallway and into the allocated room, and after apologising for the simplicity of the furnishings he assisted her into the chair usually occupied by labouring types attempting to come to grips with their consciences, then asked, 'What generated your desire to see our current barbarity abolished? I venture to suggest, if I may, that you will have had little contact with it on a personal level and I sincerely hope that a lady of your obvious education and status in society has never been exposed to the nauseating detail regarding how the execution of a condemned felon is actually conducted.'

'Spoken like a true preacher,' Mary Miller observed in a soft voice. 'But let's just say that my interest is purely from a broad moral standpoint. Since my husband died, I've taken much to reading the Bible and I am reminded of the commandment that "Thou Shalt Not Kill". If we condemn those who take the life of another in the heat of the moment, why should we not also condemn the taking of life in a cold-blooded way, as the result of an order from some judge who doesn't have to watch while it's done?'

'My sentiments exactly,' Matthew said, while making a note that this very attractive woman, seemingly still in her early thirties, was already a widow, 'but I'm still intrigued. Who was it, inside Newgate, who made you aware of my repugnance of the hanging process?'

'You close your eyes when it happens, do you not?' she said, and Matthew understood without seeking a name. It must have been either one of the hangmen, or more likely one of the jailers assisting in the grisly process, Sam Tibbins or John Tasker. Most probably the latter, since he was the friendlier of the two and had vouched for Matthew during his recent inspection of the visitors' book.

'So are you a member of one of these several organisations, of whose existence I am aware and with which I shrink to be associated because if so I would be excluded from ministering to the poor souls at their allotted time?' Matthew asked.

Mary Miller's face fell slightly. 'You are firmly committed to such a terrible vocation?' she asked. 'And are there not others — perhaps here in this very Mission — who would be prepared to lift that burden from you? I have already enquired of your superintendent and he assures me that there are.'

'Even if that be the case,' Matthew asked, 'why should I relinquish what I must admit is a very unpalatable side to my ministry?'

'Because when we begin our campaign we must take on powerful forces,' Mary explained mysteriously. 'Forces within the God-forsaken system who would seek to divert you from your self-appointed task. It is crucial that you speak as a free man with no association with Newgate, or anywhere else in which the heathen and barbaric process is practiced. Surely it would be no burden upon you to be rid of the sight of the terrible deed?'

'Of course not,' Matthew said in relief. 'On the contrary it would be a blessed release, if you assure me that others will be available in my place.'

'You have my assurance — or at least, that of your superintendent,' Mary said.

'So how large is your organisation, when and where does it meet, and how may I best be of service to it?' Matthew asked.

Mary's eyes dropped daintily down to the table. 'I must own that it is at present merely at the fledgling stage,' she admitted. 'We have no regular meeting place and it may be that in the interests of secrecy and caution we shall be required to vary them. But among the founding members, of which I am delighted to say you may be numbered, there are those well placed to broadcast our message. Your part in all this will be to add your personal experiences of being present at hangings, to record your revulsion of what you witnessed, and of course to supply us with authoritative passages from the Bible to justify our call for the process to be abolished.'

'That doesn't sound very onerous,' Matthew commented, 'and I feel that you overestimate the influence that I might perhaps be able to bring to bear on those in Parliament who must be prevailed upon to end the practice.'

'Spoken with true modesty,' Mary said as she rose to her feet and made to leave. Matthew rose from his seat and escorted her to the door, at which she paused, took his hand, and told him, 'I feel sure I've found the right man for my purpose', as she glided back into the hallway and made her way to the front door.

Matthew wondered uneasily what 'purpose' she might be referring to. It all seemed too good to be true — an elegant lady of obvious means, someone with whom he might work in order to bring hangings to an end, and an immediate termination of his need to attend them. And he still had the most pleasurable part of the day ahead of him.

'Here's your poster,' Matthew announced breezily as he entered the mortuary and handed it to Adelaide with a broad smile. She appeared to be alone and for once was not attired in her working clothes of cap, gown and boots; and as she gazed at the poster prepared on her behalf Matthew was reminded of how good an artist his sister was and how accurately she had both described and depicted Adelaide's almost sculptured jaw line, with the piercing green eyes above and the luxuriant red curls tumbling around her ears before they dropped down to shoulder height.

'I love the portrait,' she responded encouragingly, 'and the wording's about right, but I think that the final line requires some attention. Instead of the dash between my name and "Hackney", it should read "Carlyle for the Hackney Ward".'

'As you wish,' Matthew replied with a smile of his own. 'When's the nomination day, again?'

'A week on Friday,' she reminded him. 'Would you be so obliging as to accompany me to Spring Gardens that day?'

'It would be my pleasure,' Matthew beamed back and it then fell uneasily silent until Adelaide offered to make tea and Matthew nodded.

'Where's your father this morning?' Matthew asked to Adelaide's back as she bent over the teapot. 'This must be the first time that I've been in here when there hasn't been a body on that slab.'

'He's upstairs in a meeting,' Adelaide explained. 'We're hoping to extend this somewhat cramped accommodation by knocking down that wall and moving into the room next door, which at present is simply a store room. Were you hoping to see him, or were you only here to get my approval for this excellent poster?'

'Both, really. Although this is a very pleasant way to acquire a free cup of tea.'

'Your sister really is very talented. I hope some man doesn't come and flatter her over her looks and distract her from her art.'

'She is said to be a very attractive young lady,' Matthew replied.

Adelaide smiled. 'Precisely. In my experience women who are physically attractive are never taken seriously regarding their real talents. They're flattered into believing that their true value to society is to be found in their looks, and before they know what's happened they've been cajoled into marriage and child-bearing. Then they aren't taken seriously after motherhood when they try to find a market for their talents.'

'And you obviously don't wish to have your other qualities overlooked simply because you're beautiful?' Matthew blurted without thinking.

Adelaide blushed, but maintained a stony look. 'There you go, you see — you're no better than any of the others.'

'Yes I am,' Matthew objected. 'I acknowledged *both* your intellectual gifts and your natural beauty.'

'Well, concentrate on my potential as a London County Councillor,' Adelaide replied coldly. 'There will no doubt be too many men already who'll assess my fitness to govern London by means of the shape of my bosoms and the movement of my hips. Don't become one of them, else I'll be

51

obliged to find someone else to accompany me to public meetings. Our relationship is solely one of friendship and mutual respect, are we clear on that point?'

'We are indeed,' Matthew conceded, 'but you can't stop me admiring your beauty as well. I'll just keep quiet about it.'

'See that you do,' Adelaide instructed him, just as the outer door opened and Carlyle walked in.

'Ah, Matthew. I hope you haven't been kept waiting too long. And what brings you here — do you have more information for me?'

'Indeed I do. There is something interesting that I learned during a recent conversation with the church minister who attended the other two hangings on the day that Skuja took the drop.'

'And what was that?'

'Well, there were two others scheduled for execution that day, if you recall? Jack Riddings at 8 am and Joshua Zammit at 10 am? Well, the same minister was attending both of them — it seems that he knew them from his former commission as an army padre.'

'So why weren't the two men executed one after the other?'

'That's what puzzled me, but the minister — Enderby, his name is, from St. Dunstan's, in Stepney — didn't seem to see any significance in that, probably because he doesn't attend those dreadful processes as much as I do. But what was really strange — and what I hope will mean more to you than to me — was the fact that Zammit's execution was brought on half an hour early.'

Carlyle's eyes lit up as he reached for a piece of paper and a pencil from a bench to the side of him. 'So, let's see if I've got this right. Riddings went at 8am, Skuja on time at 9am and

then, from what you tell me, Zammit was dropped at what —
9. 30am?'

'Yes, so far as I can make out. Does that help at all?'

'Almost certainly,' Carlyle enthused as he began making a few rough calculations.

Adelaide was clearly eager to make a contribution. 'Body temperature?' she queried.

Carlyle nodded. 'Precisely.' He looked back up at Matthew with a broad smile. 'Do you happen to know, as a matter of practice, whether or not the hood remains on the body after death, before the doctor certifies that the condemned man is dead?'

'I've no idea — I've never looked down,' Matthew admitted.

'But it could, could it not?' Carlyle pointed out. 'Presumably what confronts the certifying doctor when they cut down the body is not particularly pleasant, so he or she will wish to minimise the process of certifying "life extinct". The swiftest way is by feeling for a pulse at the carotid artery, which is just below the jaw. The certifying doctor could reach that simply by placing two fingers under the hood, without paying any attention to the face, which would present a far from pleasing aspect, with a protruding tongue and perhaps even a bitten one.'

Matthew shivered slightly, then felt Adelaide's comforting hand on his arm. 'Welcome to our world,' she murmured reassuringly, as Carlyle stepped quickly into the tiny office behind the glass panel in the corner and began urgently sorting through the papers lying on the desk. He seemed to find the one he was seeking, read it briefly, then let out a shout of triumph before scuttling back into the main room with the paper in his hand. 'I take back all I may have thought about the incompetence of the late Dr Somerskill,' he announced, 'because they might have fooled me too, had I not been more fastidious in my work.'

'What?' Matthew asked, completely at a loss.

Carlyle waved the paper in the air. 'These are the jail records that Jennings copied for me. Your man Skuja was apparently five feet nine inches tall when he ended this life, while Zammit was only marginally taller, at five feet eleven. May I take it that all condemned prisoners go to meet their maker dressed in prison garb?'

'In my experience, yes they do,' Matthew confirmed. 'So?'

'So if I presented you with a body — call it "A" — only two inches shorter than another body which we'll call "B" and lying flat out with a hood over his head, wearing prison issue clothing, would you have any reason to doubt whether "A" was "A", or in fact "B", if I told you that it was?'

'You've completely lost me,' Matthew admitted.

Carlyle began writing on another piece of paper from the side bench. 'This may help. Here's Riddings, right? Call him "R". He goes to his death at 8am, and at sometime between then and 9am, Dr Somerskill is called in to confirm that he's dead. With me so far?'

'Yes,' Matthew confirmed as Carlyle continued writing.

'Then Skuja is dropped — denoted here by the initial "S", but of course, as we have every reason to believe, he's not dead. He's removed from the area beneath the trapdoor and is smuggled out of the prison completely. But the doctor needs to certify him as dead, so those responsible for spiriting Skuja away need another body, yes?'

'Yes, but —'

'Let Father finish,' Adelaide urged him and Matthew fell silent.

'That's why Zammit went half an hour early,' Carlyle continued. 'When they called Dr Somerskill down to certify "life extinct" for Skuja, they showed him Zammit's body, at around 9.45 at a guess.'

'But why execute him thirty minutes ahead of time?' Matthew asked.

It was Adelaide who supplied the answer. 'Body temperature,' she announced.

Carlyle nodded, then explained the significance of that for Matthew's benefit. 'Dr Somerskill was required by regulation to certify death after approximately an hour from the time of the drop. As a doctor, he would expect the body to be cooling and when shown Zammit's body at 9.45am and told that it was Skuja's, who'd been dropped at 9am, both the timing and the approximate body temperature would be right.'

'But what about Zammit's certification?' Matthew objected.

Carlyle shook his head slowly. 'You were as well to choose the Church as your vocation. Dr Somerskill was brought back in at around 10.30am, at a guess. It was his final job for the morning and he had a busy practice back in Limehouse, no doubt with patients queuing up for the privilege of lining his pockets. He's shown Zammit's body for the second time, this time of course in its true identity. He doesn't do anything other than feel the carotid pulse — certainly doesn't look at the face — and probably explains away the relative coolness of the body as natural causes such as the ambient room temperature. Since both men were of comparable heights and given that he wasn't required to provide anatomical dimensions, he simply accepted what he was told and went home for a cup of tea.'

'Then why was he murdered?' Matthew asked.

'We don't know for certain that he was,' Carlyle reminded him, 'but I cannot envisage a robbery in which a man is stabbed in the back, then left with his valuables intact, any more than I can imagine two young street arabs stabbing a man in the back.'

'All the same,' Adelaide added, 'you would be as well to take care. I've come too far to want to lose a nominator for Council.'

'I'll try not to get myself murdered before nomination day,' Matthew said drily. 'In other news, I will no longer be attending hangings.'

'That's probably all to the good, in the circumstances,' Carlyle replied, 'but what has led to that happy state of affairs?'

'A lady arrived at the Mission looking for me, because she'd heard of my aversion to the death penalty. She's persuaded me, not that I needed much persuasion, to give up my attendances at hangings — with my superintendent's approval, of course — in order to be able to join and assist a new group dedicated to campaigning for an end to capital punishment.'

'Just make sure that your political activities are focused on the LCC election,' Adelaide said frostily.

8

The next few days passed uneventfully as Matthew counted down the time before he was due to accompany Adelaide to Spring Gardens, the headquarters of the London County Council. In order to be of as much assistance to Adelaide as possible, Matthew collected all the literature he could on what she had put her name forward for and learned with some relief that she would be competing for one of two seats allocated to the Hackney Ward.

He was not so sure whether she would benefit from the formation of two political groups of councillors with broadly similar agendas that had occurred immediately after the new council had been formed. Of those, the so-called 'Progressives', with their affiliation to the Liberal Party that dominated national politics, seemed to be the most natural for Adelaide, but they had already nominated their preferred candidate, Graham Edmonds, a Bethnal Green butcher who seemed to have a large and loyal following. Adelaide's bold and nonconforming approach might serve to divert some of the popular Progressive vote from the other main contender for one of the seats for Hackney Ward, the ultra-Conservative 'Moderate' candidate Gerald Mordaunt, a self-made property developer with extensive investment interests in the West End.

The elections themselves would not be held until May, but nominations closed six weeks prior to that and it was an eager Matthew who waited in the muddy roadway outside Spring Gardens for Adelaide's coach to arrive. They had agreed to meet outside the LCC headquarters ahead of Adelaide handing in her nomination papers after Matthew had declined to be collected in the Carlyle coach at his home. For one thing, he had duties to perform earlier in the day down at the Mission, and for another he wanted to minimise any suggestion that he was merely Adelaide's hired bodyguard. They had argued the point for some minutes over supper at the Carlyle house three evenings earlier, and it had been Carlyle who had demonstrated his potential as a mediator when he pointed out to Adelaide that in the same way that she rejected any demeaning suggestion that she was not her own woman, she must allow Matthew an equivalent dignity in respect of his role in her life.

Even so, Matthew was beginning to rue his stubborn pride as the next blast of wind-driven sleet forced him to turn his back on the busy street and raise the collar of his somewhat threadbare topcoat. In the process his eyes drifted towards one of the entrance alcoves between the Corinthian pillars with which the ground floor level of Spring Gardens was adorned, and he spotted a familiar figure huddled almost out of sight under its arch. He was still trying to place the chubby countenance when its owner slipped furtively back into the gloom of the entrance and Matthew was distracted by a call from the lowered window of the arriving coach. He hurried to open the door for Adelaide, who instructed Collins to wait for her.

The formalities took a little longer than Adelaide had perhaps anticipated, when the officer who was registering her candidacy insisted on inspecting every single document that qualified her for it. But Adelaide had anticipated this sort of bureaucratic attempt to thwart her ambitions and came armed not only with the title deeds to the Hackney house in her name, but also a copy of the entry in the 1891 Census that showed her to be resident with her father in the same house.

'I admire your courage, madam,' the officer muttered as he stamped her application in duplicate and handed one copy back to her.

'My courage comes from my convictions,' Adelaide replied acidly, 'and I shall be accompanied by this strong young man, should anyone seek to exploit any misplaced belief in my feminine weakness.'

'I only hope that you haven't misplaced *your* belief in my ability to fend off any unwanted male attention during your campaign speeches,' Matthew muttered as he took her arm back down the impressive spiral staircase.

Adelaide suppressed a giggle and pulled his arm closer. 'You may be guaranteed to fight for what you believe to be yours, like any self-deceiving male,' she said.

Matthew was still wondering if that remark was a subject for rejoicing or depression as they walked back out into the street, where mercifully the sleet flurries had subsided and a wintery sun was peeking through the translucent cloud. Ahead of them a woman was scurrying towards the entrance to Spring Gardens with a parasol bent against the prevailing wind. As she came to an undignified halt in front of them, she gave a cry of recognition and grabbed Matthew's arm, pulling him towards her and planting a kiss on his cheek.

'Matthew! What a delightful surprise! Did you get my note regarding our next meeting? I *do* so hope that you can be there for me!'

Matthew remembered his manners as he introduced Adelaide to Mary Miller, but purposely omitted to advise either of them how he was acquainted with the other.

'I haven't seen your note yet,' Matthew replied, 'but I'll do my utmost to be there. What brings you to Spring Gardens?'

'Some administrative nonsense about the guttering on the upper floor of my garment factory,' Mary said. 'The tenants on the top floor are complaining about the lack of repair and some idiot in the LCC seems to think that it's my job to fix it. Anyway, I must be going.'

As she scurried off, Adelaide turned to watch her departing figure, then asked, 'Who exactly *was* that?'

'Mrs Mary Miller,' Matthew replied. 'She and I will be working together to abolish capital punishment. I believe I already told you about her.'

'I hope that this won't distract you from working with me during the council elections,' Adelaide said.

Matthew smiled. 'It won't, I promise.'

'She seemed a little forward in her manner.'

'That's just her, I suppose. Everyone's different, aren't they?'

'You certainly look different with that lipstick on your cheek. Here's my handkerchief — wipe it off before Collins sees it and reports it to Father in the belief that it's mine.'

When Matthew returned home late in the afternoon he was met at the top of the staircase leading up to the family apartments by his mother, wearing a worried frown and carrying a calling card.

'While you were out, a nice police detective called, looking for you. He'd been down to the Mission, apparently, but couldn't find you there.'

'I was up west, accompanying Adelaide when she registered her candidacy for the LCC elections,' Matthew explained in the same tone of voice he'd employed for years when justifying a late return home to his anxious mother.

'Well, he says it's urgent and to lose no time in calling in to see him. Are you in trouble?'

Matthew looked down at the card. It was from John Jennings and supplied his room number at the Yard, although Matthew had been there on a prior occasion and was fairly sure that he could find his way there again. 'It's all right, Mother,' he told her reassuringly. 'I'm assisting Jennings in a matter, along with Dr Carlyle and his daughter. He probably just wants to keep me up to date with his enquiries and learn what I can tell him from my own investigations.'

'When we gave our blessing for you to become a clergyman,' his mother grumbled, 'we didn't expect that it would involve you in police matters. I wouldn't be surprised to learn that you've been talked into something dangerous by that very attractive daughter you just mentioned. Anyway, go through to the sitting room and I'll bring you a pot of tea. Your face is all red from the wind out there.'

'More likely from passion,' Charles jibed as he appeared at the sitting room door. 'He came home in that lady's coach.'

'One of these days you'll find that your nose has stuck to that front window that you're so fond of spying on people through,' Matthew muttered as he brushed past Charles and walked into the sitting room.

The following day happened to be one on which Matthew was not required at the Mission until the afternoon, when he would be the clergyman on duty in the consultation room into which those in need of spiritual nurture or upliftment would be ushered to unburden themselves. It was therefore barely nine o'clock when Matthew presented himself at Scotland Yard, and he was halfway up the stairs to the floor that housed the detective department before he was challenged and brought back down to the reception hall and made to wait until it was ascertained whether or not Detective Inspector Jennings was prepared to see him. The man himself walked down the staircase only minutes later, apologised to Matthew for the rudeness of his uniformed colleagues, and invited him to accompany him back upstairs.

Once seated in his office, Jennings's face darkened. 'I have reason to believe that you may now be in immediate danger.'

'From what, exactly?' Matthew asked.

'More likely from "whom", although at present I have no idea, which makes matters even more perilous for you.'

'So what do you have to impart?' Matthew asked.

Jennings pushed a sheet of paper across the desk towards Matthew. 'Read that.'

Matthew did as requested and found himself looking at a copy of a crime report sheet now two days old. It came from Shoreditch Police Office and was an account of the sudden death of a man who had fallen under a bus outside the old Bishopsgate railway station, which was now used as a freight terminal. Matthew was still taking in all the details when Jennings cut into his thoughts.

'You'll recognise the name, of course, and I've left a list of names with our records office, for them to alert me if any of them featured in incoming crime reports, which are filed here when they're wired in.'

Matthew allowed his eyes to drift down the report until the name of the victim appeared. He started when he read it. 'Percy Bryant? Wasn't he the man who —?'

'Precisely,' Jennings cut in. 'The man who conducted Skuja's hanging.'

'He wasn't the normal hangman, though,' Matthew reminded Jennings. 'He was called in that morning, after the normal hangman — a man named Billington — was taken ill. At least, that's what we were told.'

'Indeed, but does that not make you suspicious?'

'You mean that Billington was bribed, or poisoned or something?'

'That I have yet to discover,' Jennings replied, 'and I'm planning to go down to Newgate this morning to enquire of him. But think about it for a moment; at the last minute they bring in a hangman who's new to the job, likely to be very nervous, and anxious to do a good job without any horrible bungles. He either won't be paying a great deal of attention to the actual identity of his victims, or he's part of a huge conspiracy to ensure that Skuja escaped his just desserts.'

'And more recently he's been clumsy enough to get run down by a bus? Why should that concern me?'

'Read the rest of the report,' Jennings instructed him.

Matthew did, then looked up sharply. 'How reliable is this eye witness? He's the bus driver, so he'd be the most eager to cover up any responsibility on his part.'

'He'd also be the best placed to see what actually happened,' Jennings reminded him. 'Bus drivers are constantly on the look-out for potential suicides, or those miserable wretches who deliberately throw themselves under the horse in order to bring a compensation claim. This one — Fred Moberly — is adamant that he saw a hand outstretched to push Bryant under the horse's hooves.'

'So even if he was murdered, how does that pose a danger to me?' Matthew asked.

Jennings frowned. 'Are you so confident in God's ability to preserve you from the wickedness of your fellow man that you've forgotten Dr Somerskill? Knifed in the back in what was made to look like the course of a robbery? Isn't it possible that all those involved in Skuja's escape from the gallows are now being bumped off?'

'But not by Skuja, because he died several weeks ago now. Poisoned, according to Dr Carlyle.'

'Obviously not by Skuja,' Jennings agreed. 'But by someone who was involved in his subterfuge and wishes to silence all those who know of their involvement in it.'

'I am not a threat, though,' Matthew assured him, 'since I had my eyes closed.'

'You may know that, but who else does?' Jennings challenged him.

Something clicked into place in Matthew's memory. 'That reminds me of something I should perhaps report to you. Yesterday afternoon I was up in Spring Gardens with Adelaide Carlyle while she registered her nomination for the LCC elections. While I was waiting for her I caught sight of someone who was looking at me, somewhat furtively I thought. At the time I couldn't place him, although the face was familiar. Now it's all come back to me, talking about those who were there on the day that Skuja escaped justice. It was John Tasker, one of the two jailers who led Skuja to the scaffold. He's a regular on the Condemned Wing and he vouched for me when I went searching for those records in the visitors' book that led me to the Reverend Enderby. Then he later told someone else that I was in the habit of keeping my eyes shut when the moment came for the trapdoor to open.'

'Who did he tell?'

'Some woman who's organising a group of people into a political organisation to call for the abolition of the death penalty. She's added me to her list and she came to see me last week.'

'Her name?'

'Mary Miller, although I don't have an address. But she's a lady of substance who owns a garment factory. A respectable widow. You wouldn't suspect her of anything, surely?'

'I suspect *everyone* until I can eliminate them,' Jennings muttered. 'If it comes to that, apart from that John Tasker who you just mentioned, there was another jailer present, wasn't there? A man by the name of Sam Tibbins?'

'That's right,' Matthew confirmed. 'If you tell me he's been done to death as well, maybe I'll take your warning with a little more concern than I'm feeling right now.'

'This is not a matter for levity, Matthew, believe me,' Jennings scowled. 'I have this feeling in my over-ample gut that someone is going to great lengths to eliminate all those who knew what actually happened when Artus Skuja escaped the fatal jerk at the end of the drop. You were there, and although I'm prepared to believe you when you say that you weren't in on it, whoever's so anxious to keep the secret won't scruple against killing a man of the cloth, believe me. He — or she — has already done for a doctor, remember.'

'I'll bear that in mind,' Matthew assured him as he rose to leave. 'May I assume that you'll be passing all this on to Dr Carlyle?'

'You may — and take care, please.'

Back at the Mission Matthew remembered something that Mary Miller had told him during their brief encounter the previous afternoon. He walked down to the board on which messages were pinned for staff and sure enough there it was. He removed it from the board, opened it out and read the brief message. *Next Wednesday, 3 pm, 27 Albion Grove, Islington. Do so hope you can attend. Warmest regards, Mary Miller.*

9

On the appointed day, shortly before the designated hour, Matthew alighted from the bus halfway up Liverpool Road and made his way on foot along Albion Grove, with its terraced late Georgian three-storied houses. Some of them had seen better days and appeared to be in imminent danger of degenerating into lodging houses, but he was relieved to see that Number 27 was largely preserved and had only three sets of residents, to judge by the bell pulls at the front door. He pulled the one that bore the name 'Miller', whose position suggested that Mary's rooms might be on the middle level, and after only a brief delay the door was opened to him by a young girl dressed in the standard black and white of a maid.

Having confirmed who he was, Matthew followed the girl up the broad flight of stairs to the second floor set of rooms, where Mary was awaiting him in the doorway, a broad smile on her face.

'Do come in, Matthew,' she urged him after dabbing his cheek with more lipstick, then leading him by the hand into a sitting room and inviting him to take the well upholstered chair near the window.

Mary perched herself on the sofa and instructed Gladys that she could now serve the tea.

Matthew looked around him as the girl laid out the tea things. The sitting room was comfortably, if modestly, furnished, with only one additional armchair apart from the sofa on which Mary had placed herself, and he was just wondering how well attended this meeting was intended to be when Mary cut into his thoughts.

'Apart from Sir Eustace Benson, you're the only one who could make today's meeting,' she told him. 'Regrettably there have been several apologies, the last of which only reached me this morning, but I have no doubt that we can use the time valuably. That will be all, thank you, Gladys.'

The maid bowed out graciously and they were alone. Matthew completed his initial assessment of the sitting room while Mary busied herself cutting a jam sponge cake on a large plate in the centre of the low table in front of her. There was a long sideboard on which was displayed a very large portrait of a younger version of Mary dressed as a bride, in the company of a man who gave the impression of being at least ten years her senior.

Mary followed his gaze and sighed heavily. 'That was my wedding day. Andrew and I were blissfully happy until he was tragically taken from me. Well, to be devastatingly honest with you, he took *himself* away from me. Took his own life, which is of course a dreadful sin in the eyes of a clergyman such as yourself, but the poor darling never got over the failure of his business. He was a pharmacist, with shop premises in Upper Street, not far from here.

'Unfortunately, as this area of London began to deteriorate socially, his business income diminished, at the same time that the pharmaceuticals that were essential as his stock in trade rose in price. There came a point at which he was obliged to declare himself bankrupt and he couldn't endure the shame. He was a proud man, you see, and a fine one who succeeded in leaving me comfortably off by means of an irrevocable trust that kept much of his accumulated wealth out of the hands of his Trustee in Bankruptcy.

'I've been a widow these three years and more and it never gets any easier. The loneliness, you know? Still, I have no doubt that in the course of your calling you're required to give what comfort you can to young widows like myself, whose anticipated enjoyment of their youth hasn't yet diminished. Do have a slice of this excellent cake, Matthew. I baked it myself, in honour of this inaugural meeting.'

'Forgive me, but I make a habit of avoiding sweet things,' Matthew explained. 'As a boy I had a tendency towards fat and I adjusted my tastes accordingly.'

'That explains why you're so fine and slender now,' Mary said as she leaned back on the sofa and crossed her legs, leaving several inches of crisp white underskirt showing over her fashionable lace-up boots. 'Are you absolutely certain I can't tempt you? To some cake, I mean. It's such a pleasurable change to have a man in the house.'

'No, I'm fine with just this cup of tea, honestly,' Matthew assured her. 'When do you expect our other member to arrive? I'm afraid I already forgot his name.'

'Sir Eustace Benson. He's a director of some railway company or other — I forget which. He also has interests in several West End stores. His principal interest, however, is in law reform and he hopes to stand for Parliament for some constituency out in Middlesex, where he resides. Hounslow, from memory. I expect him at any time. But *do* tell me more about yourself.'

'I rather assumed that you'd done some background research on me before inviting me to join your group,' Matthew replied.

Mary chuckled. 'Of course, but I was meaning Matthew West the man, not the Wesleyan preacher who closes his eyes at executions. I take it, for example, that you don't keep your eyes closed to other things — feminine beauty, for example? Do you currently have a lady friend? I know that you're not married, but a handsome fellow like you must have them chasing his coat tails.'

'No, regrettably not. I'm afraid that the price one pays for doing God's work is financial penury, so I cannot even consider seeking to interest any lady in a future with me.'

'Surely, if the lady who captures your interest has financial means of her own, then your problem is solved, is it not, if she finds you physically alluring?'

'I'd never thought of myself in those terms,' Matthew admitted.

Mary gave him a coquettish look from under lowered eyelids. 'You obviously don't know what women look for — particularly if they have the financial means with which to support a suitable marriage partner. But did I not see you recently in the company of a most alluring young lady, outside the LCC building in Spring Gardens?'

'Miss Carlyle? Yes, you did, but I am only assisting her in her ambition to gain election to the LCC. She's in a different social league entirely from me, I regret to say. Her father is a leading surgeon and she's the legal owner of a most magnificent house in Hackney, where she hopes to serve as a councillor.'

'She's obviously very courageous and determined, as well as beautiful,' Mary commented. 'There's never been a woman on the LCC so far as I'm aware, since very few can meet the property qualifications, as do I as well, of course. Perhaps a lady so committed to a cause might wish to join our campaign against capital punishment? In return I'll do what I can to rally some of my propertied friends to vote for her.'

'I've never enquired as to her opinion of the death penalty,' Matthew told her, 'although I know that her father is against it.'

'Then she probably is also. You would do well to cultivate her, Matthew. She's beautiful, she's monied, she's intelligent and ambitious. She's in her mid-twenties, at a guess — just the sort of age at which a woman's body begins to long for a child.'

Matthew was conscious that his face was slowly reddening and he sought urgently for another topic to discuss. 'Did I understand you to say that you have a garment factory?'

'Yes indeed, just around the corner from here. A two-storey building in Hemingford Road. I own the entire property. I acquired it after my late husband died and I was obliged to revert to my old trade. I was his assistant in the pharmacy for several years, you see, but before that I managed a garment factory for a friend. We specialised in ladies' undergarments — corsets, stays, underskirts and the like — and I was sufficiently well proportioned in those days to be able to model each new garment that we manufactured for the West End stores, bearing the exclusive "Tulip" label. But I'm a little fuller in the figure these days, so perhaps I should lay such ambitions to rest.'

'You continued in the same trade with the money left to you by your husband?' Matthew asked, a little hot under the collar.

Mary nodded. 'Yes, I was most fortunate. I employ six women in a collection of rooms on the ground floor, while enjoying the rental income from the family on the upper floor. Except they seem to have taken to complaining about the state of the roof. Anyway, forget them. I'm happy to say that my undergarments are still on display in some of the finest and most exclusive stores in Regent and Bond Streets. That's how I come to know Sir Eustace Benson, of course — he's a great admirer of them.'

'It has to be hoped that he arrives soon,' Matthew observed, for more reasons than one.

Mary nodded. 'It's most unfortunate that we've been kept waiting. Are you absolutely certain that you don't want any of this cake? It's a shame to let it go to waste, and I've already had two slices.'

'Really, I'm quite content with a second cup of tea, if I may,' Matthew replied.

Mary duly obliged. 'However, the late arrival of Sir Eustace doesn't mean that we can't make a start,' she suggested. 'I had hoped that we might begin to pencil out a few ideas for slogans to put on brochures that we can distribute everywhere where they're likely to be read. Libraries, clubs, railway stations, cafeterias and so on. The cost of printing them will be a major outlay, of course, but perhaps your father could oblige with a trade price quote.'

'You really have researched my background well, haven't you?' Matthew said.

She nodded. 'But there's much more about you that I'd like to get to know, Matthew.'

Matthew felt apprehensive as well as uncomfortable. 'One obvious Biblical text we might employ is the Commandment "Thou shalt not kill",' he persevered.

Mary rose from her sofa, walked to a writing desk at the side of the room and returned with a pad and pencil. This time prior to sitting back down on the sofa she contrived to lift the hem of her straight skirt to knee height, along with the underskirt, as if adjusting them so as not to crease them when she sat down and Matthew looked away modestly from the flash of stockinged knees that this revealed.

For the next hour or so they considered various Biblical texts that Matthew came up with and Mary conscientiously listed them all, although Matthew began to gain the impression that she was losing interest as time progressed and the carriage clock on the sideboard struck four pm.

Gladys entered deferentially in order to remove the tea things and Matthew took the opportunity to suggest that perhaps he had better consider making his way home. Mary seemed quite amenable to this suggestion, and with a feeling that somehow he hadn't lived up to her expectations, he followed meekly behind Gladys as she ushered him through the front door of the apartments and down the staircase to the street door.

He thanked her as he stood outside the entrance, adding, 'It's a pity that Sir Eustace wasn't able to attend as planned.' When Gladys looked blankly back at him, Matthew explained. 'Sir Eustace Benson? He was meant to be here also, was he not?'

'Never 'eard of 'im, beggin' yer pardon, sir,' Gladys replied meekly. 'I was told ter expect only you. "Tea for two", the Mistress said.'

With that, she closed the door, leaving Matthew feeling a little foolish. But by the time he'd joined the queue for the southbound bus he was also feeling suspicious and somewhat relieved that he'd refused any cake.

10

Matthew breezed into the mortuary after the most perfunctory of knocks on the door, with a broad smile on his face and carrying a sizeable cardboard box. Even the fact that Dr Carlyle appeared to be in the process of extracting internal organs from a man laid out on the slab in front of him didn't dampen Matthew's mood as he looked across at Adelaide. 'Here's the brochures for tomorrow. Two hundred of them, hot off the press and ready to impress the voters.'

'Don't touch that box until you've finished with that zinc solution,' Carlyle called out, and Adelaide nodded her compliance.

Matthew wandered over to the bench at which she was stirring a blue/black mixture in a small metal pot and looked over her shoulder. She looked back at him. 'Did Father advise you of his finger impression experiment?'

'He did indeed,' Matthew confirmed, and turned when he heard Inspector Jennings correct her.

'Strictly speaking it's *our* experiment. And good morning to you, Matthew.'

'Sorry, but you have a habit of hiding in a corner in here and I didn't notice you when I first came in.'

'Probably because your eyes were elsewhere,' Jennings replied with a smirk and a nod towards Adelaide's back, 'but police officers such as myself develop the art of being invisible, lurking in quiet corners wherever they may be found. May I say how relieved I am to find you still alive?'

'What did he mean by that?' Adelaide asked as she turned sharply to look at Matthew.

He shrugged. 'Inspector Jennings has this theory that I'm next on some killer's list, but don't worry — I plan to still be alive tomorrow and I'll be here by one o'clock at the latest.'

'What's happening tomorrow?' Carlyle asked as he slipped an entire lung into a metal dish by his side. 'Could you weigh this please, Adelaide? Preferably *before* you apply the zinc solution. I've examined under the fingernails and as I suspected this man was scrupulous in his grooming. Still didn't prevent him from departing this world gasping for breath, if the state of the left lung's anything to go by. He gives no sign of having engaged in manual labour, but his lungs are in the same state that I see with those who shovelled coal for a living. But his clothes reek of tobacco, so perhaps that's what converted his lungs into what look like shrivelled prunes.'

'What's his story?' Matthew asked of Carlyle, but it was Jennings who supplied the answer.

'Collapsed and died at the dinner table in his club up west. His widow's trying to blame the lobster bisque, but I think that the answer may lie in the cigar case in his waistcoat pocket. Boodles *will* be pleased.'

'Who's Boodles?' Matthew asked.

Adelaide giggled as Carlyle replied, 'His club. Adelaide, you didn't answer my question about tomorrow.'

'It's the day when all the candidates for the LCC elections make a short speech on the steps of Spring Gardens,' Matthew explained.

'Since when was your name Adelaide?' Adelaide demanded as she turned to address her father. 'It's not until two o'clock and I don't suppose I'll be there for longer than an hour at most. I've already written my little speech, with some help from Matthew, so I can stay on later this evening if you need me to. Added to which, I'll be here with you in the morning, dressed ready for the pantomime. I'll just have to make sure not to get any zinc solution on my best green costume. Green for "a cleaner, healthier London".'

'Talking of zinc solution,' Carlyle replied, 'you might wish to show young Matthew here how we take finger impressions.'

'Just stay where you are, Matthew, and prepare to be enlightened,' Adelaide said as she took the container from the bench, along with a blank piece of paper that had a name written on it, then walked back to the cadaver on the slab and grasped it firmly by its cold limp left wrist. She lifted the hand and dipped in into the inky solution and then pressed all five fingers firmly down on the paper, leaving what looked like a child's drawing of five brussels sprouts on its otherwise pristine surface. Then she repeated the process for the right hand, placing the inked impressions from that below those on the left, labelling them 'L' and 'R' accordingly.

Finally she placed the paper face upright on the bench to dry, with firm instructions to Matthew not to touch it. Then she turned to address Jennings. 'You now have Herbert Lansbury in your records, although he doesn't look as if his life was dedicated to burglaries.'

'Talking of low criminals,' Matthew asked of Jennings, 'how are you going with your investigations into the death of Mr Skelton, who was previously Mr Skuja?'

Jennings shook his head. 'A bit of a dead end at present, I'm afraid. The pun was, of course, intentional, although your responding laughter was optional. But of course it just got worse, with three of my obvious suspects eliminated.' When Matthew looked puzzled, Jennings explained. 'Skelton — as we have to call him, since that was the name he died under — appears to have been poisoned. We can assume that there was a reason for that, since according to the doctor here the poison was not a soured batch of beer, or a bad oyster, but a very specific substance. So someone was out to get him, clearly. Since he was officially dead, in his capacity as Artus Skuja, we can only assume that whoever poisoned him knew that he was still alive and calling himself "Skelton". The only ones who knew that he'd survived the hanging were the executioner Bryant — now dead — and the jailers Tibbins and John Tasker. Even if we assume that Dr Somerskill wasn't originally in on the plot, for some reason he was also murdered, suggesting that he'd perhaps tumbled to what had gone on and unwisely said so. But both Bryant and Somerskill died *after* Skelton, which suggests that whoever was trying to silence those who knew of Skuja's escape from the gallows was someone *other* than Skuja. Someone trying to cover up their part in it.'

He paused and looked at Matthew in amusement. 'I've lost you, haven't I?'

'I'm afraid so,' Matthew admitted. 'Tell me again — or perhaps in a different way.'

'Allow me,' Carlyle intervened, then looked at Matthew while wiping his bloodied hands on a napkin he took from the corner of the slab. 'Think of it this way,' he urged Matthew. 'Skuja cheats death and there are five people who know that, apart, obviously, from Skuja himself. That five includes you, of course, so let's give you the benefit of the doubt and bring that number down to four. There's the executioner Bryant, the two jailers Tibbins and Tasker and the doctor, Somerskill. Then it seems that someone gets nervous about the fraud being revealed and sets out to eliminate all those who knew about it, or may be *suspected* of knowing about it — which again includes you, of course.'

'I hope it doesn't,' Adelaide responded without thinking, then reddened slightly as she glanced fleetingly at Matthew in order to assess his reaction. 'After all, my plans for the elections are well advanced now.'

'Whether it does or not,' Carlyle continued as if nothing had been said, 'Inspector Jennings was more correct than he realised when he said that his primary suspects are diminishing. The most obvious person wishing to cover up Skelton's re-emergence into the community in his new identity would of course have been Skelton himself. But the careful process of eliminating those who knew about it didn't occur until *after* his death, which raises an enormous unanswered question regarding the motive for it.'

'Clearly, someone who wishes to eliminate all knowledge of *their* part in it,' Matthew mused.

Carlyle looked across at him. 'You really *have* put my methods into practice, haven't you?'

'Which is why I recently warned Matthew to be very careful,' Jennings chimed in. 'If we assume that he isn't the one committing these murders — for two reasons, one of which is that he had no idea of the trick performed under his very nose, and the other being his closed eyes — then there can be only two possible suspects left. That's the two remaining jail staff, Sam Tibbins and John Tasker. If by some lucky chance one of these is croaked in the near future, then we have our man. The survivor.'

'You can't seriously be hoping for another man to be murdered?' Matthew challenged him, shocked and morally outraged. 'And why are you assuming that two jail drudges were capable of arranging something as sophisticated as a man being hanged and still evading death? I've met them both and neither of them is exactly a genius. If they had half a brain between them, they wouldn't be working in Newgate.'

'He has a very good point, Inspector,' Carlyle said. 'Admittedly, he's using a process of logic that he learned from me, but that doesn't detract from its validity. We cannot avoid the possibility that there was another person pulling the puppet strings from outside — someone who now wishes to cover their tracks.'

'That doesn't make a lot of sense, with respect, Doctor,' Jennings argued back. 'The only reason why anyone might be killing those involved is in order to protect their own involvement in the business. Which implies that someone was threatening to spill the beans. But whoever that was would be known to the murderer and they wouldn't need to murder the other two under the suspicion that they were the one about to peach.'

'You've lost me again,' Matthew complained.

Jennings sighed. 'Assume for the moment that it was Dr Somerskill who was threatening to go public, or was perhaps seeking to blackmail the others, one of whom decided to silence him. Since his identity was known to the murderer, why did they then need to go on to silence Percy Bryant?'

'I see your point now,' Matthew replied, 'but it raises another confusing point — for me, anyway. If someone *was* threatening to reveal what happened, whether for the purpose of blackmail or whatever, wouldn't that require them to reveal their own part in it? Think about it for just a moment — did someone threaten, in all seriousness, "Give me money or I'll reveal to the authorities that I was a party, along with you, to a serious perversion of justice that allowed a man to evade the gallows"?'

'He has a point there too, Inspector,' Carlyle chuckled and even Adelaide was nodding admiringly.

Jennings was far from happy. 'So you think there may be someone else entirely behind it, do you? Someone else whose identity I don't have a clue about, who was organising things from outside the jail? And why?'

'As for the who,' Matthew reminded him, 'you will recall my reporting back to you that a woman called "Bridget Dempsey" had visited Skuja three times in Newgate? Have you got any closer to identifying her, since she may be just the person you're looking for?'

Jennings made a frustrated noise and shook his head. 'Have you any idea how many Irish bog-trotters are called "Dempsey"? And how many of them name their female offspring "Bridget"? You didn't even give me an approximate age for the woman, who may have adopted an assumed name anyway, but even if she didn't I could still fill two buses with women of that name without looking north of Commercial Road.'

'All the same, she fits the bill for someone from outside, making the necessary arrangements for Skuja to dodge the noose,' Matthew insisted.

Jennings nodded with a look of despair.

'And don't forget also,' Carlyle added, as if determined to pile on the agony, 'that Skuja was a blackmailer. If you go back through those whose premises he conveniently torched before he was caught, he may have prevailed upon one of those to make the necessary arrangements.'

'Even I can see a flaw in that, with respect,' Matthew offered deferentially. 'If Skuja had been blackmailing me, I'd have been delighted to see him take the drop. The last thing on earth I'd want was for him to cheat the gallows.'

'A good point,' Carlyle conceded, 'which unfortunately takes us back round in the same circle. So perhaps whoever poisoned Skelton, as he became, was someone he attempted to blackmail *after* he assumed his new identity. Someone who had nothing to do with his staged hanging. Do we know who his associates were after he re-emerged into the daylight?'

'We looked carefully into that, as I mentioned when I first brought you his corpse,' Jennings reminded him. 'We can't be certain that he committed any more arsons as "Skelton" and his only regular visitor in his final few weeks, according to his neighbours in Spitalfields, was a young woman who they assumed was a high-class prostitute. She never stayed long, apparently.'

'So you're no further forward in investigating Skelton's life after his rebirth?' Matthew asked gloomily.

Jennings shook his head. 'However,' he told the assembled company, 'I'm working my way through the list of those whose premises we believe he burned down at their request when he was Skuja. Most of them are obviously reluctant to admit that they paid him to do it and there are still some who're hanging onto the insurance money because the company can't prove deliberate arson, so it's not easy.'

'But surely, they'd want to see Skuja dead, after he double-crossed them and started on the blackmail after burning their premises down?' Matthew said.

'That's one of the reasons why it's not so easy,' Jennings grumbled. 'But it's just possible that after he survived the execution he went back to blackmailing those he'd been blackmailing before. Someone who'd survived the insurance company enquiry and still had a lot to lose if the truth came out. They're probably wallowing in ill-gotten gains that Skelton wanted a share of.'

Matthew hesitated for a moment, then decided to ask anyway. 'At the risk of overburdening you, could I ask you to look into the background of someone I heard of only yesterday, who I suspect may not exist?'

'If you think it's important,' Jennings sighed. 'Who is it?'

'A man called Sir Eustace Benson. I was told that he was a director of a railway company, with substantial shareholdings in several West End stores and a potential candidate for a Middlesex Parliamentary constituency.'

'I'll see what I can find out,' Jennings promised as he closed his notebook. 'I now I must be going.'

'As must I,' Matthew announced. 'I really only came in here to deliver these brochures to Adelaide and I have things to do down at the Mission.'

'Don't forget that you have things to do tomorrow at two o'clock,' Adelaide reminded him.

'I'll be here by one o'clock,' he promised. 'Unless the friends of Skelton get to me first.'

11

Adelaide swallowed hard as she stood in line and looked down apprehensively at the curious faces of the moderate crowd in the roadway beneath the temporary wooden platform that had been erected for the benefit of the nominated candidates for the upcoming LCC elections. The platform itself was already beginning to wobble slightly from the sheer number of would-be councillors who had been invited to address the crowd that they almost outnumbered, many of whom were obviously newspaper men. She looked down into the front row and smiled palely at Matthew, who was grinning up at her encouragingly and nodding his support.

It seemed to take forever, as each nominee for a seat on the LCC promised the electorate the earth, the moon and a few stars thrown in for good measure. There would be full employment, the appreciative crowd were promised by speaker after speaker, in addition to a five and a half day working week in London factories, in the docks, in the shops and in the fish-gutting yards and tanneries. There would be plentiful sanitary housing at low cost to those renting them, with no restrictions on the size of the families that could be housed in them, regular street cleaning, a bathing beach on the north bank of the Thames and another free hospital on the north side of the city, to avoid the inconvenience of travelling down to Whitechapel in order to receive treatment at the London Hospital that was already overcrowded and allegedly insanitary. In short, everything that Adelaide had been intending to promise — except that she actually intended to deliver it, if it came within her power to do so.

Finally it was Adelaide's turn and as her name was called out, she stepped forward, to a chorus of shouts, wolf-whistles and the odd obscene suggestion. She let fly before the crowd had even ceased baying.

'Did it never occur to any of you small-minded morons that women might also possess brains? Brains that can be combined with compassion for the ordinary family, for the struggling worker and his six children?'

It suddenly fell silent and Matthew allowed himself a silent groan. He and Adelaide had spent several evenings in her Hackney house going over what she would say in this all-important first address to the electorate and this was nothing like the wording that Matthew had tactfully suggested.

She was meant to sympathise with those standing before her, to explain how well aware she was with the problems that confronted them daily and to promise them to work tirelessly to improve the conditions of everyday life in those areas of the overcrowded city that previous local government bodies had systematically ignored. Instead, she was giving the impression that she was a loud-mouthed and slightly vulgar harridan.

'That's telling them,' came a voice in Matthew's ear just as a soft hand was laid gently on his arm. He turned to see Mary Miller smiling at him just before she planted a kiss on his cheek.

'Are you back here in connection with the need to fix the roof on your factory premises?' Matthew asked.

Mary shook her head and pulled him closer. 'No, I'm here to support your lady friend — what's her name again — "Abigail"?'

'Adelaide,' Matthew corrected her.

Mary nodded to confirm that she'd heard him above the rising din of hecklers who were beginning to give Adelaide a rough time of things. 'She's got guts,' Mary told him, 'and we women have to stick together in a man's world. I had hoped to bring a few friends along with me, to add to her support, but I don't see any of them here yet.'

Matthew transferred his attention back to Adelaide when he heard her all but screaming at some newspaper man who must have said something to reignite her wrath.

'Typical remark from a man! I *may* be the only woman on this platform, but that must surely tell you something, you brainless pencil pusher! What it should tell you is that women are under-represented where it matters — in the very place where the conditions under which they have to live are at the mercy, and under the condescending control, of cretins like you!'

This provoked a good deal of laughter from the crowd and a loud shout of 'Well said, lady!' that almost deafened Matthew.

Adelaide looked down at where he was standing, then frowned slightly when she realised that the shout of support had come from Mary. This did nothing to improve her temper and the remainder of her allotted ten minutes was swallowed up in a heated exchange with several press reporters who seemed to be enjoying the responses they received whenever they goaded her into some other intemperate outburst that they faithfully noted down for tomorrow's early edition.

The other candidates had remained politely on the platform to hear the speeches from their rivals, if only to openly sneer at them. However, once advised that her allotted time was up, Adelaide stormed off the platform to a few remaining jeers and hurried over to where Matthew was still standing in a huddle with Mary. 'I may as well give up now,' she grumbled.

Mary shook her head. 'Far from it, my dear,' she attempted to console her, 'it's about time that someone like you took a stand.'

'You remember Mary Miller, of course?' Matthew said. 'She's the lady who's working with me to abolish capital punishment. We met just here on the day that you handed in your nomination paper.'

'I am here to offer you some support,' Mary said. 'I have a lot of lady friends who're qualified to vote and I had hoped that they'd be here today, to hear what you had to say.'

'Thank God they weren't,' Adelaide shuddered, 'since I made a complete fool of myself up there.'

'You were too easily provoked,' Matthew ventured to suggest, but was withered where he stood by an angry glare from Adelaide.

'Who *wouldn't* have been? Those utter imbeciles who pass for newspaper reporters were obviously bribed by my opponents to get me going on an issue that's so important to me. Once I started, I forgot all those fancy words you put into my head and they proved as useless as praying to God.' She turned to Mary. 'Thank you for your support, but I really need to be addressing groups of men, since theirs is the citadel that I need to be storming.'

'Well *there's* one you can attempt to convert,' Mary announced as she looked over Matthew's shoulder and called out to a portly gentleman on the front row, listening intently to yet another speech from the platform. 'Eustace!' she shouted.

The man waved and pushed his way over, raising his bowler hat politely to Adelaide.

'Matthew,' Mary cooed, 'let me finally introduce Sir Eustace Benson, who was unfortunately unable to make our meeting the other day. Eustace, please say hello to the Reverend Matthew West and Adelaide ... er ...'

'Carlyle,' Adelaide replied coolly. 'Adelaide Carlyle. You probably missed what was supposed to be my candidature address just now.'

'Far from it, dear lady,' Eustace beamed as he took her hand, leaned down and kissed it. 'I thoroughly enjoyed it. Quite the liveliest piece all afternoon, so far anyway.'

'For all the wrong reasons,' Adelaide muttered.

'That depends what your intentions were, my dear,' Eustace replied somewhat patronisingly. 'Some of these journalist chappies require to be put in their place, don't you know?'

'I know only too well,' Adelaide replied stonily, 'but I was supposed to be announcing my intentions for the future welfare of London should I be elected, not doing an impersonation of a woman on a fish gutting quay down in Limehouse.'

'Time enough for that, surely?' Eustace persevered, earning a snort from Adelaide.

'If I haven't ruined my chances already and *if* I decide to stay in the contest. Come on, Matthew, if you can tear yourself away from your own group of supporters.'

She turned sharply and headed off at a stiff pace to the street around the corner where Collins was waiting with the coach. Matthew was hard put to even keep up with her and they were both breathless as they climbed into the coach.

Adelaide ordered it to the Shadwell Mission.

The atmosphere inside the coach was chilly in the extreme as it trundled down Northumberland Avenue on its way to the Embankment and Collins's preferred route into the East End, via the Temple, Blackfriars and Monument. Matthew desperately wanted to say something to lift Adelaide's spirits, but was fearful of incurring a tongue-lashing and — even worse — a declaration that his services were no longer required for her election campaign.

Eventually, it was Adelaide who broke the silence. 'Precisely how many people were present at that meeting you had with Mary Miller, always assuming that's her real name?'

'Just me and her, as it happens. And she's genuine. She's a widow who was left enough money to own her own garment manufacturing business and she has a respectable enough residence in Islington.'

'You've been there?'

'Yes, that's where the meeting was.'

'Just you and her?'

'Yes, as I already mentioned. Sir Eustace Benson was meant to be there, but for some reason or other he failed to attend.'

'A reason that you haven't been given?'

'No — look, Adelaide, what exactly is the purpose of all these questions?'

'You're being had, Matthew. Either that, or I am.'

'What on earth do you mean?'

'Well, whoever that old idiot was back there in Spring Gardens, he was no peer of the realm. What name was he using again? Sir Eustace Benson?'

'And you determined that how, precisely?' Matthew asked, growing increasingly irritated.

'I'm my father's daughter,' Adelaide replied, 'and I notice things.'

'Such as?'

'Well, for a start he had rough workmen's hands. What were you told he does for a living?'

'He's a director of a railway company and has major shareholdings in several West End department stores.'

This provoked a hollow laugh from Adelaide. 'Unless he stokes the coal into one of his own locomotives, or unloads goods into his own retail warehouses, there's no explaining how a man of his apparent status in life has hands like a coal heaver.'

'You may have imagined that,' Matthew argued, reluctant to admit that he himself had doubts about Sir Eustace Benson until he actually met him less than an hour ago, 'since you only held his hand for a second or so and you were wearing gloves.'

Adelaide smiled knowingly. 'The thing about wearing gloves of the fine quality of mine is that you feel every rough ridge on the hand of a person who holds it, if only momentarily. Then there were his shoes.'

'It was raining earlier,' Matthew reminded her.

Adelaide nodded. 'Indeed it was, which explains the spattered mud. But underneath that were scuff marks, highlighted even more strongly by the way that the mud formed a different surface on the scuff marks. A gentleman of the quality that "Sir Eustace" was pretending to be would have thrown those shoes out months ago, or at least handed them down to his footman or someone. He'd certainly never venture abroad in them.'

'So what purpose do you think Mary Miller had in trying to deceive me about being well connected? Matthew asked.

Adelaide shrugged. 'I can think of two reasons, only one of which gives me cause for concern. The first is that she's out to impress you, either to persuade you to join some political cause that is far from as enhanced as she'd have you believe, or because she's out to lure you into her bed.'

Matthew burst out laughing. 'That second reason is quite preposterous!'

'It wasn't my second reason,' Adelaide replied stiffly. 'It was the second part of my first reason and I may say that you could do worse, if she really *does* have money to recommend her, rather than just a rapidly fading beauty.'

'Your second reason?'

'She's trying to undermine my election campaign.' She saw the look of amusement on Matthew's face and grew more heated. 'Don't look like that! She was there when I registered my candidacy and she was there today. For all we know she's been recruited by one of my rivals — which means just about every man hoping to prevent a woman winning a seat on the LCC — and is doing what she can to ruin my chances. By distracting you with her feminine wiles, for example.'

'She doesn't distract me,' Matthew protested, although it came out without conviction.

Adelaide's eyes narrowed. 'Don't for one moment misunderstand me, Matthew. I don't give a damn whether she won you over during your meeting in Islington, but I *do* take it badly if you're being used to undermine my political campaign. Perhaps I should find someone else to accompany me to future meetings. After all, you were useless at this one.'

While this last part of the conversation had been taking place the coach had come to a halt. As Matthew sat staring at Adelaide in sheer disbelief and misery the flap in the roof of the coach opened and Collins called down, 'We're at the Mission, Miss Adelaide.'

'Well — off you go and do something useful for a change,' Adelaide instructed him curtly and Matthew angrily threw open the coach door and descended into Cable Street. Calling out to Collins to 'Drive on', he stomped through the Mission's front door and threw himself into a seat at the rear of the chapel, his favourite place for seeking solace and inspiration. Only this time he was seeking answers for the injustice that seemed to have suddenly descended upon him.

As he calmed down, he tried to see things from Adelaide's perspective. Her first venture onto the hustings had been a disaster and she had exposed her Achilles heel to the entire world; it was only necessary to say something derogatory about women and she would explode like a firework. Quite what Matthew could be expected to do in order to preserve her from herself was anyone's guess and it was certainly unfair for Adelaide to have criticised him for failing to come to her rescue. That was just Adelaide trying to deflect the blame from herself, which was only human nature.

But the comments about Mary Miller and Sir Eustace Benson were another matter altogether. His first reaction had been to laugh at the suggestion that Mary Miller's real agenda was to seduce him into some sort of sexual relationship, but then he thought back to certain ominous aspects of the 'meeting' that she had contrived, to which she had invited him as the only attendee. She had been somewhat forward with her bodily gestures, displaying undergarments seemingly out of carelessness.

Then there were the references to articles of female underwear and her pleasure at posing in them. Were all these pieces of behaviour aimed at seducing him? If so — why? Surely not to distract him from his appointed task to assist Adelaide in the LCC elections; apart from the fact that Adelaide was fighting a losing battle from the very start, she'd done her chances no good at all at her first attempt, so why would Mary need to add further sabotage?

So why did Mary Miller want to draw Matthew into a close, and perhaps immoral, relationship? If she just needed a man, they would be easy enough to come by in the circles in which she moved, in which discretion was guaranteed and money was no object. There had to be some reason why Mary needed Matthew and he could only hope that when that time came it would not push Adelaide further away from him.

Then there was the curious Sir Eustace Benson. The man who was not even expected at the meeting that Mary had convened in her house. Why had Mary maintained the pretence that Sir Eustace would be attending? Was it intended simply as a cover for what she hoped to seduce Matthew into when they were alone? Or was Mary attempting, as Adelaide had suggested, to promote the impression that her anti-hanging group was larger and more influential than it really was?

There was perhaps some truth in Adelaide's assertion that they were being taken for a ride and Matthew could only await developments. His priority task must be to restore his relationship with Adelaide, with whom he found himself more in love with every passing day.

Carlyle's eyebrows rose when Adelaide stormed back into the mortuary with the facial expression of someone who'd just missed the overnight train to Edinburgh. She threw her bag down on the side bench and began making tea in stony silence, then made a half-heartedly attempt at an apology when she realised that her father was not alone.

'Sorry, Inspector, but you were lurking in the corner as usual and I didn't see you.'

'May I take it that the event didn't go off to your liking?' Carlyle asked tactfully.

'Don't ask!' Adelaide reached for the tea caddy. 'Would you both like some tea, since I'm making some anyway?'

'Not for me, thank you,' Jennings replied. 'I'm only here to collect some more finger impression sheets for storage at the Yard.'

'Well, while you're here, could I ask that you investigate a couple of people for me?' Adelaide said.

Jennings nodded as he extracted his notebook and pencil.

'The first is a so-called titled gent,' Adelaide told him. 'He calls himself "Sir Eustace Benson", but I have reason to believe that he's a fake.'

'So does Matthew, funnily enough,' Jennings told her. 'He asked me to make the same enquiry that you just requested, if you recall.'

'I'd forgotten,' Adelaide admitted. 'Anyway, I'm sure he didn't ask you to also investigate the background of a lady called "Mary Miller". I use the term "lady" loosely as I believe that she's trying to seduce Matthew for some dark purpose of her own, possibly connected with reducing my election chances even more.'

Jennings took his departure and Adelaide poured tea for herself and her father. In the uneasy silence, Carlyle decided that some fatherly advice was called for.

'Be honest with yourself, Adelaide. What's upsetting you more — the thought that someone's trying to undermine your electoral bid, or the possibility that another woman's got her eyes on Matthew?'

Adelaide's face set in a determined stare back into her father's eyes. 'The former, of course. Why should I be jealous over Matthew?'

'Just a thought,' Carlyle replied quietly.

'Just so that we understand each other, Father, I hold no candle for Matthew. Perhaps the day may come when a man steals my heart and exposes the weaker side of me, but that man will not be Matthew West.'

12

Matthew sat staring gloomily out of the sitting room window down into the street, wondering what life would throw at him next. He seemed destined to sink slowly down into a pit of despondency while all those around him were being favoured with good news.

The first had been the excited announcement by his sister Caroline that her first pen and ink drawings of prominent London buildings had been accepted for a series of special articles in the *Evening News*, which was seeking to outsell its competitors by featuring local landmarks from all over the busy metropolis. The entire family had gathered round to congratulate her and her proud father had made her a gift of a set of pens. But even that was overshadowed by what Matthew's brother Charles had announced over supper earlier that evening.

'I'm proud to be able to advise you all that Miss Susan Byfield has graciously consented to become Mrs West,' he beamed across the rabbit pie in the centre of the table. 'Matthew, you'll be marrying her to me. You'll agree to do that, won't you?'

Matthew shook his head sadly. 'I'm afraid I can't, unless you propose doing it inside the Mission.'

'Why on earth not?' George West demanded.

'I feel sure that Miss Byfield would wish to commit matrimony with my dear younger brother somewhere other than in the Assembly Room in the East End Mission. I don't yet have a church of my own, do I?'

'Can't you borrow one?' Caroline asked, to general laughter that turned her face pink when she realised that this must have been a stupid question.

Matthew smiled kindly at her as he replied, 'It doesn't work that way, I'm afraid. Certainly, if I had a church to which I was attached I could "borrow" another one, as you put it, by conducting the service in another church within the network. But it's a question of status within the Wesleyan fold, I'm afraid. I *have* done a few weddings down at the Mission, but they were in the main for local girls who'd unfortunately fallen into the family way, one of them only last week — to a merchant seaman from Jamaica who was setting sail on the afternoon tide on the morning that I joined them together in what I hope proves to be holy matrimony. I've also done a handful of funerals for destitutes in the Workhouse. But until I have a church of my own I couldn't offer you a wedding venue other than the Mission in Cable Street, which would hardly be likely to appeal to a fashion-conscious bride like Susan Byfield.'

'So how come you've never been promoted?' Charles asked.

'Has it not occurred you that they might wish to keep me at the Mission?' Matthew asked. 'Not everyone's cut out for ministering to the lowest in society and I've heard it said more than once that I have a gift for it. Perhaps it comes from having to tolerate a younger brother,' he added with a sideways smirk at Charles. 'Congratulations, by the way. I'm sure that Susan will make you very happy and I shall of course pray for blessings for you both, even though I won't be able to conduct the service.'

Now, as Matthew dejectedly watched the rain drops spattering into puddles in the roadway outside, lit by the dull glow from one of the occasional gas lamps that lined the narrow street, he was reflecting ruefully on the fact that he couldn't even officiate at his own brother's wedding. He would be twenty-eight on his next birthday and he was living on the meagre stipend that was the basic income of everyone ordained into the basic level of the Wesleyan Church. Even were he to be granted a 'living' as an Assistant Minister in a chapel somewhere, it would bring in as much income as a lowly lawyer's clerk, although it would carry with it a rent-free house conveniently located close by, in order that he might more efficiently carry out his duties.

By comparison, his brother Charles was a businessman with prospects — a director of the family printing business established by their father and remunerated according to the level of the annual profits, which in recent years had been growing healthily. Matthew was also a notional director of the same enterprise and enjoyed a small income for doing absolutely nothing. At his request, the money was paid into a trust account which at the last count was approaching a credit balance of some sixty pounds.

It was hardly a fortune and these days barely enough for two months' rent for a decent house in a respectable London suburb. The sort of suburb acceptable to a lady of breeding who wouldn't be content to be cramped into a two-roomed cottage designed half a century earlier for a single clergyman with a live-out housekeeper. Not that the lady of breeding that he had in mind appeared to be in the remotest bit attracted to him; if anything the friendship between himself and Adelaide that he had hoped to fan into something warmer seemed to have plummeted back into the depths from which he had striven for weeks to extract it. It wasn't his fault if Adelaide had made a complete pig's ear of her first address to potential voters, but she was clearly intent on blaming him for it, and the chance encounter with Mary Miller had only made things worse.

While it was almost laughable to consider for one moment that Mary might be out to thwart Adelaide in her bid to become the LCC's first woman councillor, Mary's arrival on the scene had clearly complicated Matthew's bid to win Adelaide's affections. He might be well advised to give Mary a wide berth until after the elections, not that her ambition to launch a campaign against the death penalty seemed to have risen far from the concept stage, so a delay of a couple of months would probably make no difference one way or the other.

Matthew reached the Mission the following morning, and had just shaken the rain from his topcoat as the door to the superintendent's office opened from the inside and Livingstone called his name and beckoned him inside.

Once he was seated, Livingstone had wasted no time in getting to the point. 'Are you familiar with West Ham?' he asked.

'I know where it is, obviously, but little more. Why?'

'We opened a Wesleyan chapel there a few years ago.' Livingstone consulted a note at his elbow before adding, 'Green Street, if it helps.'

'Not in the slightest, I'm afraid.'

'Well it's been doing very well, thanks to the excellent work done among the recently expanded working-class community out there by Herbert Rawlings. So well, in fact, that we had to expand it earlier this year. Now Herbert Rawlings has passed away and his young Assistant Minister Peter Grimwade has been left holding the baby, so to speak. He's a very able man and it seems to be the wish of the Trustees that he be offered the main ministry. That leaves a vacancy for a new Assistant Minister and I've been asked to approach you to see if you might be interested.'

'Asked by whom, if I might enquire?'

'I'm not authorised to tell you.'

'Why me?' Matthew asked.

Livingstone smiled. 'You and I have had our differences, and there have been times in the recent past in which your capacity for attracting publicity to yourself has presented us with difficulties, but your ministry among the very poor, the very weak, and the downright depraved has been outstanding. The people of West Ham are very similar to those here in Shadwell — in the main they are labourers in the docks and on the railways. There are large families living in poor accommodation, and Peter Grimwade's strengths lie more in his liturgical grasp, so he would benefit from someone at his elbow with your common touch. It's an opportunity for you to take the next step on the career ladder within our humble movement and become an Assistant Minister.'

'You wish me to make formal application in accordance with the normal competitive process?'

'That won't be necessary if you're interested. You'll certainly need to apply formally, but if I can convey your interest to the Trustees, then that application should become a mere formality, given the recommendation from me that will accompany it. You could move in by the end of the month, should that be convenient, and in the meantime I can relieve you of most duties here while you take time to familiarise yourself as much as possible with the area.'

He saw the hesitation in Matthew's face and frowned slightly. 'I expected to see more elation in your countenance, Matthew. You're well overdue a step up on the ladder and it's to your considerable credit that you've obviously so taken to the salvation of souls here in Shadwell that you haven't given any thought to your own career progression. Opportunities like this come only rarely and while I hesitate to suggest the hand of God guiding your actions —'

'Forgive me if I seemed a little distracted,' Matthew interposed, 'but it's just that I've recently given a commitment to a good friend of mine to assist them in a matter of considerable importance.'

'You mean Mary Miller and her abolition group? Surely you could continue to work with her in that while moving only a few miles to the north-east of here?'

'No, not her. Someone else, who has hopes of improving life here in the East End for those who choose to live their lives in accordance with the law,' Matthew hedged, unwilling for some reason to go into any further detail regarding Adelaide.

Livingstone's frown had not disappeared as he nodded towards the door. 'Perhaps you need time to further reflect on the wonderful opening that has been offered to you. And how you might best serve God. I'll divert any deserving causes while you spend some time in silent meditation, either in the chapel or in your private room. And remember your solemn vow to the Almighty, to serve him in all His glory and to work in all His ways. This is no time for misguided humility, Matthew. Off you go.'

Alone in the empty consultation room, Matthew was in a quandary. This new opening he'd been offered would obviously be a welcome boost to his career and would provide him with the means to be able to officiate at Charles's wedding to Susan Byfield. And if he rejected this generous offer, which of course reflected well on how he was regarded within the Wesleyan movement, then he would be doing his chances no good for any future living that might emerge and which he found more appealing.

But it would hardly be likely to appeal to Adelaide, and he risked pushing her further away if he moved to West Ham. For one thing, wherever his new church was located the duties involved would render it impossible for him to stand alongside her as she fought the almost impossible battle to break the male monopoly of local government. Perhaps best, on balance, to leave well alone.

He looked up as a shadow darkened the open doorway, then rose hastily to his feet to welcome Mary Miller and show her to the seat across from his behind the battered old desk. She smiled effusively and held out her gloved hand for him to take as he lowered her into the same chair she had occupied when she'd first approached him regarding the newly-formed movement against the death penalty.

'I hope I'm not intruding on your thoughts,' she said. 'Only you seemed to be in another world just then.'

'No, it's fine,' Matthew replied with more enthusiasm than he felt. 'I was just wondering what I should best be doing next to help those around me.'

'Like your delightful young lady's almost hopeless attempt to become a London County Councillor?' she asked without any obvious malice.

'She's not my "young lady".'

'But you'd like her to be? A woman can tell these things. But she's still only young, and probably doesn't even know her own mind yet. Unlike we more mature types; unfortunately some of us only learn what it is that we really enjoy until it's no longer available. Young Miss Carlyle would be well advised to grasp the opportunity for eternal bliss while it's still available in such a magnificent form as yourself.'

'What can I do for you?' Matthew asked with an abruptness that was almost rude.

The smile on Mary's face faded slightly as she replied, 'I've been giving some thought to who we might invite to join our select group. I have enough promises of support from gentlemen of commerce and those in minor political office. In addition, of course, I have your very powerful moral guidance and Biblical knowledge. But I feel that we need more backing from those who reach out in our material world to remind us of the duty we owe to our fellow men. In short, more clergymen like yourself.'

'I know very few of them, I'm afraid,' Matthew admitted. 'The Church of which I'm a member doesn't enjoy a particularly public profile.'

'That isn't quite what I had in mind,' May replied as she reached into her bag for a notebook and pencil. 'You obviously attend these dreadful displays of human brutality that some are wont to describe as "justice taking its course" and it has sickened you to the point at which you're prepared to take a stand against it. There must be others of your calling upon whom it's had the same effect and I was wondering if you might point me in the direction of a few. If we could collect some written protests against the death penalty from men of God that we might publish in booklet form and distribute around the libraries, bookshops and so on, this might help to get our message across.'

Matthew thought for a moment. 'There's only really one other church minister I can point you towards. Some time last year I had occasion to be one of two ministers who officiated on a dreadful morning when three men were executed in the space of three hours. I only ministered to one of them, but the other two were attended by the same minister, who'd known

101

them during their army days, before they went to the bad. His name is Thomas Enderby and he's the Curate of St Dunstan's Anglican Church in Stepney. A likeable enough chap and I'm sure that if you agree to take sherry with him he'll give you a suitable piece.'

Mary smiled appreciatively as she wrote down the details, then looked back up at Matthew. 'We really *must* get this campaign launched, if you're not too busy fussing around Miss Carlyle in her election ambitions. I apologise for the fact that you had an almost wasted journey to my house the last time, but we might think in terms of holding something more grand, perhaps in a private room in some fashionable hotel. I'll get word to you in due course.'

Matthew was in the process of assuring her that he'd be sure to take the time to attend, whatever plans Adelaide might have for him, when there was a knock on the door and it opened to reveal a somewhat embarrassed looking Superintendent Livingstone. There was a woman behind him in the doorway and Matthew realised with a start that it was Adelaide.

'Please forgive the intrusion, Mr West,' the superintendent said, 'but there's a lady here who insists on seeing you immediately. She says that it's a matter of the utmost importance and immediate urgency, so I took the liberty of interrupting. I do hope that it didn't come at an inconvenient moment.'

'As it transpires, I was just taking my leave anyway,' Mary said as she put her notebook and pencil back in her bag and rose from her seat. She smiled back at Matthew, then looked at the superintendent. 'If you weren't already aware, you have a fine man here.' With that she swept from the room, pausing only to award Adelaide a triumphant smile as she passed her.

No sooner was she out of the room than Adelaide rushed in, red in the face. 'What was *she* doing here?' she demanded. 'It doesn't matter. Sam Tibbins has died. He was fished out of the river this morning, where he was found face down after a fatal swim two days or so ago. Inspector Jennings is out in the coach and we're taking you back to the hospital for safety. We think you could be next!'

13

'You surely don't expect me to abandon my work at the Mission and go into hiding?' Matthew protested as he sat with Dr Carlyle, Adelaide, and Inspector Jennings around the teapot in the cramped 'office' space at the rear of the Mortuary. 'I should by rights be there now, tending to the spiritual needs of any of those who require consolation, comfort and hope for the future.'

'Like that dreadful Mary Miller?' Adelaide asked acidly. 'The only comfort *she* needs from you would require you to take your clothes off.'

'That's not only unworthy of you, but also factually incorrect,' Matthew objected.

Jennings intervened. 'She's not all she seems, Matthew, and we have grounds for believing that she's evilly disposed towards you.'

'When are you going to get around to telling me about poor old Sam Tibbins?' Matthew said.

'He was fished out of the Thames at Gravesend,' Jennings told him, 'but we believe that he drifted down on the outgoing tide. He was stranded on a mudflat as the water receded and a couple of watermen found him. Dead a couple of days, according to the doctor here.'

Carlyle nodded. 'I didn't have him brought down here, you'll be delighted to hear. For one thing, he wasn't smelling too good and for another, the cause of his death was quite obviously a massive blow to the back of his head.'

'How do you know it was Tibbins?' Matthew asked.

'He'd been reported missing by his wife,' Jennings replied, 'and he had a distinctive mole under his left eye. The widow fainted when confronted with the remains and when she came round she had to be sedated. You don't react like that for strangers.'

'So that leaves John Tasker as your main suspect, from what you said a few days ago,' Matthew said.

Jennings nodded. 'I've got men following him and watching his every move. If he comes within yards of you, we'll buckle him.'

'You're the only one left from that morning when Skuja was hanged,' Carlyle joined in. 'If we assume that the guilty party who organised that and is now seeking to cover their tracks, is systematically eliminating everyone who could point the finger at them, then not only has Mr Tasker unwittingly revealed his own identity, but he's also pointing the searchlight at his next victim. That's why we think you should lie low for a while.'

'Impossible!' Matthew protested. 'I have the souls at the Mission to think about and my work towards abolishing the death penalty, not to mention assisting Adelaide in her election campaign.'

'Thank you for putting me last in your order of priorities,' Adelaide replied acidly, 'but perhaps you might consider promoting me up your list of worthy causes when you learn more about the lady calling herself Mary Miller.'

'You mean that isn't her real name?'

'It is,' Jennings told him, 'but it's a name that sprang to mind when Miss Carlyle asked me to investigate her background.'

Matthew looked pointedly at Adelaide as he asked, 'And why precisely did she do that?'

Adelaide flushed slightly as she provided the answer. 'There was something about her that didn't quite feel right. She was obviously sucking up to you and —'

'And you were jealous?' Matthew asked with an impudent grin.

'Don't be ridiculous!' Adelaide retorted, growing a deeper shade of pink. 'I thought that she might be trying to undermine my election prospects at the request of one of what I suspect are several lovers. She's got sexual promiscuity almost etched into the several lines in her face under all that cosmetic camouflage.'

'The claws are well extended, Matthew,' Carlyle chuckled, 'so perhaps best to avert your eyes.'

'Do you want to know what I learned, or don't you?' Jennings asked with irritation. 'Because if not I've got other calls on my time.'

'Sorry — go on,' Matthew invited him.

'As I said, the name rang a bell and I believe I already mentioned, on a prior occasion, that Artus Skuja came to grief when a man for whom he'd performed an arson was overcome with remorse and peached on him to the police.'

'Yes, I remember,' Matthew replied. 'I also seem to recall that the reason for his remorse was that innocent people were killed in the fire.'

'That's right, the family living above the pharmacy premises that he owned, but which was in dire financial straits.' The sudden memory of a recent conversation in a second floor apartment in Islington flooded into Matthew's brain and he was hardly surprised when Jennings concluded, 'That man's name was Andrew Miller and he employed his wife Mary in the pharmacy.'

'Yes, she told me all that herself when I met with her at her residence,' Matthew admitted, to a snort of derision from Adelaide. 'I hadn't put two and two together,' he continued, ignoring her, 'because of course I didn't have access to the details of Skuja's crimes.

'And you were too beguiled by her feminine wiles,' Adelaide muttered.

Matthew was about to deny that hotly when Carlyle came back into the conversation. 'Presumably this Mary Miller didn't tell you that the fire was lit deliberately and that innocent people died in it?'

'Of course not,' Matthew confirmed. 'She didn't even mention a fire. Only that her late husband's business had gone bankrupt and that he'd committed suicide from the shame of that.'

'You see what a liar she is?' Adelaide said.

Carlyle raised his hand. 'Please let Matthew continue,' he urged her.

Jennings asked his next question. 'How did she explain her current apparent wealth away?'

'She said that her husband had been putting money away into an irrevocable trust fund that his Trustee in Bankruptcy couldn't touch.'

'An obvious lie,' Jennings said, 'since the bankruptcy laws don't work in that way. She must be funding her lifestyle in some other way.'

'So Mary Miller's husband Andrew was one of those who employed Skuja to set fire to his shop for the purpose of an insurance fraud?' Matthew asked, and when Jennings nodded, he added, 'And that led to his suicide? If so, why wouldn't Mary want to see Skuja hanged? Why would she be involved in his escape from the gallows, which is what you seem to be implying?'

'I have no idea,' Jennings admitted, 'but does it not strike you as too much of a coincidence that she's now hanging around you, pretending to be interested in the abolition of the death penalty?'

'You think she might be trying to find out if I've been investigating the mystery of Skuja's apparent resurrection?'

'I'm just alerting you to her background, that's all,' Jennings insisted. 'For my money, the real villain behind all the killings designed to cover up what really happened is the one who survived them all — Tasker. As I said, I've got men following every step he takes from now on.'

'But you're not having Mary Miller followed?' Adelaide asked.

Jennings shrugged. 'Why should I?'

'Because she may have evil designs on Matthew, that's why,' Adelaide replied in a raised voice.

'And Adelaide doesn't want to lose the man who's going to fight off the other males attending her election meetings,' Matthew added.

'That's not the only reason,' Adelaide admitted in a small voice, going slightly red again. 'I mean, you're too nice to be murdered.'

'Can I get that in writing?' Matthew asked with a cheeky grin.

Adelaide ignored him and turned to Inspector Jennings. 'What else have you learned about Mary Miller, Inspector?'

'There wasn't much more to learn, really,' Jennings told her. 'Before she married Andrew Miller she was a costume designer, it seems, and a textile model. You can still see artists' impressions of her modelling corsets and undergarments in catalogues.'

'She also mentioned that during our meeting at her house,' Matthew told him, provoking a genteel snort from Adelaide.

'And what exactly did *that* have to do with capital punishment?' she demanded hotly. 'You were being seduced, Matthew, admit it. We only have your assurance that you didn't fall for it.'

'You have my word as a man of God,' Matthew replied, hot under the collar. 'But I'm now prepared to concede that capital punishment may not be the foremost thing on her agenda. It falls into place alongside what you observed about that shady character pretending to be Sir Eustace Benson. Inspector, did you check out this Mary Miller or Eustace Benson in order to find out if they had any criminal history?'

'Naturally,' Jennings replied. 'I can tell you that there's no such person as Eustace Benson, knighted or otherwise, so Adelaide was probably right when she suspected him of being an actor down on his luck. As for Mary Miller, there's nothing known about her, even under her maiden name of Byfield.'

Matthew looked across at Adelaide, whose eyebrows had risen at least an inch as she asked, '"Byfield". Isn't that your brother's —?'

'Yes,' Matthew confirmed as his spirits plummeted. 'But presumably there's more than one family with that name. Inspector, what can you tell me about the Byfields?'

Jennings extracted his notebook and flicked through his notes. 'Not a lot, really. The father died quite young, it would seem from what I noted down here, and he left his wife and two daughters comfortably off. The elder of the two daughters had been adopted, apparently, and she seems to have disappeared from view, while the younger one was last heard of in Farringdon Market, running the greengrocery business that her father had founded. She doesn't seem to have come to our attention at all.'

'The younger daughter with the greengrocery business,' Matthew asked hoarsely, 'is her name by any chance Susan?'

'Yes,' Jennings replied with a look of surprise. 'Do you know her?'

'Not half as well as my brother does,' Matthew replied with a groan.

Adelaide reached out to touch his arm in a gesture of support. 'Mary Miller was Mary Byfield before she got married?' Adelaide asked in order to leave no room for doubt. Jennings confirmed that this was the case and Adelaide kept going. 'She was adopted, you said?'

'Also correct,' Jennings confirmed, 'seemingly from the old Homerton Workhouse. That's in Hackney,' he added.

'I know it well,' Carlyle nodded. 'I occasionally attend there and I know that they encourage adoptions, because I have to examine children from time to time and certify them disease-free before they're taken out by worthy families.'

'When was this?' Adelaide asked.

Jennings went back to his notes. '1870,' he replied. 'According to the records, she was nine years old at the time.'

'So she'd be thirty-two or so now,' Adelaide calculated quickly in her head. 'That seems about right.' She turned sadly to speak to Matthew. 'You'll have to tell Charles, obviously.'

'Tell him what, exactly?' Matthew asked, the anguish written across his face. 'That his fiancée's step-sister was once married to a man who hired a criminal to burn down his shop premises and killed a family of five in the process? That the man then committed suicide because he couldn't live with the guilt? How does that reflect badly on Susan?'

'I didn't suggest that it did,' Adelaide argued. 'I just think that Charles should know, that's all.'

'In case he wants to change his mind about marrying Susan, you mean? My brother has all sorts of faults — as do we all — but he's not that shallow. Susan and Mary aren't even blood related, but even if they were why should Susan be punished for what her sister did?'

'And what if Mary finishes up being arrested for all these murders?' Adelaide challenged him.

Matthew shook his head. 'We've no evidence that she was involved in any of them. All we know at this stage is that she married a weak man who stooped to crime to ease his financial worries, then topped himself when other people died as a result. If anything, that's to his credit, if you ignore the mortal sin of taking his own life.'

'There's still the matter of where her wealth's coming from,' Jennings reminded them. 'She may have been in league with Skuja after he became Skelton, sharing in an ongoing blackmail business. There must have been some fires that he set for which he didn't pay the penalty and he may well have continued blackmailing those he'd been employed to "assist" in the little matter of those fires.'

'Pure conjecture,' Matthew argued.

Jennings nodded. 'I agree with you on that score, but many a criminal has been brought to book as the result of some dogged investigator's conjecture.'

'So you'll continue to investigate Mary Miller?' Adelaide asked.

Jennings nodded again. 'Obviously, but you'll also appreciate that I need to continue giving priority to Tasker, since he's a more likely suspect. Anyway, I need to be going. As for you,

Matthew, if nothing will dissuade you from going about your daily life as normal, keep a close lookout behind your back.'

He duly departed and Carlyle moved back into the main mortuary in order to bring his fingerprint records up to date with those belonging to Sam Tibbins, recorded for posterity in Thames mud on an old envelope from Carlyle's jacket pocket.

Adelaide and Matthew sat staring at each other enquiringly and it was Adelaide who gave in first. 'You *will* tell Charles, won't you?'

'I suppose I have to, but I don't want to do anything to impede his happiness. I know I'm an old-fashioned sort of person, but I truly believe in the joy that awaits those joined in holy matrimony, in which I also still believe, despite what you hear these days about broken marriages.'

'There's nothing wrong in being old-fashioned, Matthew,' Adelaide replied softly as she leaned forward and kissed him lightly on the cheek. 'That's for being such a lovely, genuine person. And to give you the courage to tell Charles what you know.'

After Matthew had left, Carlyle insisted on making more tea, then invited Adelaide to leave off sweeping the mortuary floor and sit and talk to him.

'First of all,' he said, 'do you wish me to enquire at the Workhouse about this Mary Byfield? I know that they'll give me access to their records if I ask nicely, but do you really want the information that I may unearth?'

'Yes, of course,' Adelaide insisted. 'Why would I not?'

'Because it may cause Matthew even more distress, for two reasons. First of all, for the possible implications for his brother's feelings for her step-sister. Then regarding the extent to which he's been taken in by this Miller woman. I was thinking deeply while Inspector Jennings was telling us her life history and a horrible thought struck me.'

'That she had some exposure to pharmacy, you mean?' Adelaide asked with a knowing smile.

Carlyle chuckled. 'I've trained you too well, obviously. You made the same connection that I did.'

'Clearly Skelton — or "Skuja" — was poisoned by someone who had access to a foxglove extract and who knew its properties when converted into digitalis,' Adelaide said. 'While it's medically prescribed for those with a heart condition, it can be fatal if administered to those who don't need it and no doubt all bottles containing it are clearly labelled to that effect. Also, those giving it out over the counter in a chemist's shop would be trained to warn the patient of the dangers of overdosing, so Mary Miller would have every reason in the world for knowing how to bump someone off with it, perhaps by slipping it into their tea. Then compare her with Jennings's preferred suspect, a jailer called Tasker and which of them is the more likely to have poisoned Skelton with digitalis?'

'But you didn't warn Matthew against taking tea with Mary Miller — why not?' Carlyle asked.

'If she meant to kill him, she's had every opportunity already, particularly when he unwisely accepted her invitation to visit her house. What could be more innocent than to offer him tea? But she didn't poison him, so I can only assume that she has some other purpose for him. One thing I seem to recall is that she persuaded him to cease attending hangings at Newgate, not that he seemed to require much persuasion on that score.'

'Perhaps you were right when you alleged that she simply wants to seduce him,' Carlyle suggested.

'Dear God, I hope not. He's only a naive young man and I imagine that he's never known a woman. She's very attractive.'

'That's something else I wanted to talk with you about,' Carlyle told her. 'I've obviously seen you grow from a baby to the delightful young woman that you've become and I think I know you as well as anyone can claim to. Do I detect that you're beginning to warm towards Matthew?'

Adelaide blushed and looked down at the floor. 'I don't really know *how* I feel about him, Father. I just know that I'm happier when he's around and I feel safer. I never had a brother, so I don't know if the feeling's just sisterly or not.'

'Let me ask you this, then,' Carlyle persisted. 'If he were taken from you tomorrow — let's say by this Miller woman — how would you feel?'

'Empty. Cheated. Lost. Do you think that means I love him?'

Carlyle took her hand and kissed it. 'It just means that you have to treat him more kindly, if you want to keep him, sweetheart. Sometimes you allow your wild temper to break loose on the one person who should be spared it. If you think you may love him, be more gentle with him.'

14

'Mother said you wanted to see me,' Charles West announced as he walked into the sitting room where Matthew was waiting for him with a solemn face. 'Have you finally found yourself a church where you can perform our wedding ceremony?'

'That's one thing I need to tell you,' Matthew replied sadly. 'Sit down for a moment.'

'Only for a moment. I'm off to the theatre with Susan — we're heading up west, to the Savoy, to see "The Mikado". It's reckoned to be a first-class jape.'

'This will only take a moment,' Matthew assured him, 'but I need to get it off my conscience.'

'You're finally prepared to admit that it was you who broke my tennis racket when you were in your final year at school?'

'A little more serious than that, I'm afraid. I've been offered a church of my own, but I intend to turn it down.'

'Why on earth would you do that?'

'I don't imagine that West Ham would have appealed to you as a wedding venue.'

'So you turned down a promotion just because you wanted the venue to be suitable for Susan and me? How very noble of you, big brother. But that still leaves us without a church and I suspect that there were other reasons, knowing you.'

'There were, but we needn't go into them.'

'Something to do with the lovely Miss Carlyle?'

'Yes, if you must know. I couldn't continue to assist her in her ambition to get a seat on the LCC while fulfilling the duties of an Assistant Minister.'

'So now that you've unburdened yourself, I'm free to leave?'

'No, there's something else.'

'Well, make it snappy. I've got a coach arriving shortly, to collect Susan from home.'

'It's about Susan, I'm afraid.'

Charles seemed to lose some of his customary cheery bombast as he took the seat he'd previously disdained to sit in. 'What is it — have you discovered that we're long-lost cousins or something?'

'Not quite, but what do you know about her step-sister — the adopted one, Mary?'

'Nothing, apart from the fact that she was a few years older than Susan. According to her the parents were told that they couldn't have children of their own, so they adopted Mary. Then, as apparently often happens in such cases, along came Susan. But what's all this about?'

'So Susan hasn't had any recent contact with Mary?'

'They haven't met for years. I think Susan was only in her early teens when Mary left home and went to live outside London somewhere. Susan never speaks about her, so what is all this about?'

'I hate to have to tell you this, Charles, but I have good reason to believe that Mary is in London and may have been involved in a very serious criminal offence. She married a pharmacist and they had a shop in Islington that burned down one night.'

'These things happen, but so what?'

'The fire was deliberately lit and a family of five living above it perished.'

'And you reckon that it was Mary Byfield who lit it?'

'No, not exactly. By then she was married and using her married name of Miller. It was her husband who paid someone else to light it.'

'And Mary wasn't involved? So why are you telling me this?'

'I didn't say she wasn't involved and it's more complicated than that. I just wanted to prepare you for the shock if and when you found out.'

'But so what? It had nothing to do with Susan, did it?'

'Not so far as I'm aware.'

'Then why should it concern me? If I went out and murdered someone, would it reflect badly on you?'

'Not directly, but the family name —'

'The woman's name is "Miller", or so you just told me. Who's going to connect that with "Byfield"? In a few months time Susan's family name will be "West" anyway — and if you'd get a shake on and find yourself a church, instead of mooning around that Carlyle woman, then you could play a leading role in bringing that about.'

'I'm glad you see it that way, Charles, and I applaud your loyalty to Susan. It does you great credit.'

'Not half as much as you giving up a promotion in order to get your lady friend into politics. When does Adelaide give her next public address, by the way? Susan and I thought we might pop along — could be quite entertaining and she probably needs a few supporters.'

'She's planning on using one of those "Speakers' Corners" in Victoria Park tomorrow. That's in Hackney, where she lives and where she's hoping to get her seat on the LCC. And she'll be bringing along a few of her fellow believers.'

The next morning, Matthew and Charles carried a picnic hamper up a grass slope in Victoria Park and laid it down under the giant oak, a few yards away from the permanent stone platform on which those making use of Speakers' Corner stood to harangue their audiences. The speakers were traditionally those who had taken to announcing the End of the World, the Second Coming of Christ, or the advantages to be enjoyed as the result of consuming various dubious health tonics, so there was an equally lengthy tradition of hecklers who entertained themselves on otherwise uneventful Sundays by lobbing verbal missiles, orange peel and grass clods at them.

Once the huge hamper had reached the ground, Adelaide's best friends and political accomplices Constance Wilberforce and Emily Peveril set about their appointed tasks. In Constance's case it was the unpacking of the hamper, while Emily spread the large blanket over the recently scythed grass.

As meat pasties, salmon sandwiches and various items of fruit emerged from the hamper, to be distributed among those attending to support Adelaide, Matthew was reminded of the parable of the feeding of the five thousand. Then once again the burden of what he had undertaken to do clouded his thoughts and he went over in his mind how he intended to introduce Adelaide.

It took a certain type of preacher to engage a crowd and this was one of Matthew's great strengths. He was equally familiar with the drunks and hecklers who mocked him every Saturday as he sought to convey the word of God to the market crowd passing along Wapping High Street, so they would pose no difficulty for him. But political dogma was new to him and he had thought long and hard about how he might gain — and hold — the attention of those who might form the usual semi-circle around the concrete plinth, then hand over to Adelaide, in order that she could get her message across to those in Hackney that she hoped to be representing on the LCC in a few weeks' time.

Adelaide walked over and handed him a large glass of orange juice. 'For your tonsils,' she told him encouragingly.

'Have you got something to lubricate my thoughts?' he asked.

She shook her head. 'If I had, I'd be using it myself. I'm a little apprehensive, to be perfectly honest with you.'

'If you're as human as I believe you to be under all that facade,' Matthew grinned back at her, 'then you'll be as downright frightened as I am.'

'But you're used to this, surely?' she queried.

He nodded. 'In a sense, yes. But selling the word of God to Saturday drunks is a whole lot different to addressing the respectable worthies of Hackney on political issues.'

'Leave the politics to me and just get me an audience. That's your job and it won't get any easier while we stand here thinking about it. And leave the hecklers to Constance and Emily — they've come armed for the task.'

Matthew took a deep breath, walked onto the square of concrete and began. 'Ladies and gentlemen, I have great news for those of you who feel oppressed, downhearted and without a voice in this busy world that we inhabit.'

'Yer mean the missus is plannin' on leavin' me?' came the voice of the first man to halt, on his way to the public toilet further up the drive.

'No — I bring you glad tidings of someone who cares for your future welfare,' Matthew replied. 'You *and* your friends — if you have any.'

'Another Bible thumper,' the man replied with a soured expression, 'but at least this one has a sense of humour. I'm off fer a piss, but I'll be back.'

'I normally speak only of the love and boundless mercy of God, it's true,' Matthew continued unabashed, 'but in addition to that today I can offer another blessing for you and your families as you struggle with the conditions in which you are obliged to live and work.'

By this stage his audience consisted of two men, three women, a small boy and his dog, but others were passing by and he raised his voice to attract them into the immediate foreground in front of his square of concrete.

'Do you really feel that the recently formed London County Council has improved your lives? Did you expect more from them? Have you had occasion to complain about something — garbage collecting in smelly abandonment in the streets, horse dung in steaming piles where it's been left to fester, rats over-running the sparse acres of land on which your children are required to play? And did anyone care, or do anything about it?'

The crowd was rapidly swelling and several of the men who had drifted in looked as if they might be local constituents with a voting right, so Matthew moved to his final point.

'At long last someone has come forward who is willing to represent your interests on the London County Council. But she needs your support, your commitment and your all-important vote when it matters. Ladies and gentlemen, I give you Miss Adelaide Carlyle!'

There was a total silence as Adelaide thanked Matthew with a nervous smile and stepped up in his place. She looked out over the crowd of twenty or so, including her own supporters, cleared her throat and smiled broadly. 'That's right, I'm a woman. Anyone have any objection to that before I begin to advise you what I plan to bring to the work of the LCC if elected?'

'Apart from an improvement in the scenery down there?' asked a man who sounded more educated than the usual hecklers, so who might prove to be more of a nuisance.

Constance moved down the small crowd to stand immediately behind him, while Matthew sidled into place alongside the man, a tall individual who looked altogether too well dressed for a Sunday flyer of kites or launcher of boats on the nearby pond.

'Thank you for that compliment,' Adelaide smiled graciously back at him. 'So you don't believe that the LCC will be any the worse for having a woman on board who cares deeply about the state of this city?'

'What happens when you have babies?' the same man asked, to which Adelaide replied, somewhat frostily, 'I don't intend to, in the near future.'

'Well when you decide to, here's my card,' the man replied, to raucous laughter from the growing crowd. Constance's face set like drying cement as she extracted the long hatpin from the inside of her jacket lapel and lunged forward with it in her hand. The man gave a startled yelp as it dug into his buttock and turned to glare accusingly at Constance.

'Did you just stick something in my arse?' he demanded.

Constance smiled sweetly and retorted, 'Of course not — I'd hate to stem the flow of your thoughts.'

The man turned round completely as he became the source of everyone's amusement and loomed a clear six inches above Constance's head as he raised his left arm, only to have it grabbed and twisted backwards by Matthew, standing next to him.

'Let's listen to the lady, shall we, my friend?' he whispered menacingly as the man dropped his arm, glared at Matthew, then stormed off, bumping into several onlookers in his haste to leave.

Adelaide smiled at Matthew and Constance, silently mouthed her thanks and continued. 'There goes a man who obviously doesn't care about the squalor on our streets. The filth, the uncollected garbage, the rats, the crime, the slum housing.'

'An' yer gonna change all that, is yer?' demanded a rough looking workman on the back row of what was now a crowd of almost forty.

'I shall certainly be doing my best to do so,' Adelaide replied. 'At least, I shall make it my business to ensure that those who are supposed to be improving conditions in this city are actually confronting the issues, rather than spending their days in endless lunches at the expense of those who pay to keep them in power. I mean you, the ratepayers, of course.'

'We've 'eard all this afore,' the workman complained. 'Just because yer've got a fine set o' tits, 'ow does we know that yer'll not turn out like all the rest? Tell us that, then.'

'I'm standing for a seat on the LCC *precisely* to bring an end to those empty promises,' Adelaide insisted. 'I work closely with my father, who's a surgeon at the London Hospital and I've seen first-hand the consequences of poor sanitation, inadequate public health and rampant disease spread by rats and other vermin.'

An hour later, Matthew was tucking into an egg sandwich and enjoying another glass of orange juice, while all those around Adelaide were congratulating her on her inspiring performance. Matthew noticed his brother Charles engaging her in a private conversation, during the course of which she looked Matthew's way and appeared to frown. He thought nothing of it until the hamper was being repacked, the blanket was being folded by Constance and Emily, Charles and Susan had strolled off hand in hand towards the bandstand in which a brass band was giving it their all, and Adelaide sidled up to him.

'How do you think that went?' she asked eagerly.

Matthew smiled. 'If the faces of those who were actually listening are anything to go by, you've already got twenty or so votes.'

'Only another seven hundred or so to go then,' she grinned ruefully. 'But thank you for your support and assistance, even if you *did* have to rough-handle that awful man near the beginning.'

'He was threatening Constance,' Matthew explained, then chuckled. 'Mainly, I think, because she'd stuck a hatpin in his situpon.'

'I'm so lucky having friends and supporters like you,' she beamed. 'But was it really necessary for you to give up a promotion in order to continue assisting me?'

'My brother has a big mouth,' Matthew commented. 'But to answer your question, yes it *was* necessary. If I were to become an Assistant Minister I wouldn't be able to continue working in your cause, because I wouldn't have enough spare time.'

'And what if I get elected, then decide to give it all up to get married, then what?' she asked.

Matthew reached into his waistcoat pocket and grinned. 'When you decide to do so, here's my card.'

15

Carlyle smiled appreciatively at the lady who brought him the Adoption Register for Homerton Workhouse, only a mile or so from where he lived in comfort with his daughter. Suppressing his guilty feelings he turned the pages until he reached 1870, then adjusted the glasses on the end of his nose as he began to read the entries in faded ink. Finally he found the one relating to the nine-year-old girl certified as 'bodily fit and disease-free' by a predecessor ahead of her being adopted by Mr and Mrs Byfield, with an address in Hoxton. He pondered for a moment after recognising the name, then swore under his breath.

Thanking the staff for their assistance and promising to make himself available for any future medical services that might be required, he hurried back out to the coach, where Collins was waiting, opening the door as he saw his employer emerging swiftly from the front doors.

'Where to, sir?' Collins asked.

'Back to the hospital first, to collect my daughter,' Carlyle instructed him, still slightly breathless from his discovery. 'Then on to Scotland Yard.'

'That must be the fastest response I ever got to a call-out,' Inspector Jennings said as he trotted down the Yard's main staircase towards Carlyle and Adelaide while in the process of slipping into his topcoat.

'We didn't receive any call-out,' Carlyle told him. 'We're here to advise you of something *very* important regarding your enquiries into the Skelton case.'

'That can wait,' Jennings replied. 'We're off to a suspicious death in Stepney. The coach should be at the door by now and I think I may need your assistance on this one. Either that, or I'll be wasting your valuable time.'

'Not for the first time on either count,' Carlyle puffed as he raced to keep up with him across the chequered floor of the entrance lobby and down the front steps into the coach.

'St Dunstan's Rectory, Stepney,' Jennings ordered the coach driver. 'Put some urgency into it — when you get into the area, it's on the hill, they tell me.'

Carlyle leaned back against the headrest, partly to regain his breath and partly in order to recall the name from his copious memory. 'The Reverend Enderby — the other clergyman present at Newgate on the day that Skuja did his vanishing act.'

'Now seemingly the *late* Reverend Enderby,' Jennings confirmed.

'And why the police interest?' Carlyle asked.

Jennings replied, 'He was on my list of possible future victims, so I "flagged" his name at the Yard, just in case.'

'And why might you be wasting our time?' Adelaide asked.

'Because it may be a straightforward death. According to his wife — sorry, his widow — he clocked out with a heart attack. But then so, officially, did Arthur Skelton, until we handed him over to you.'

'And why couldn't you just bring the body to the mortuary?' Carlyle asked.

Jennings tapped his nose. 'I want you to go over the room where he died.'

'Why? Do you suspect foul play?'

'The man was in his mid-thirties, given to healthy pursuits like a long walk along the river bank each morning and not inclined towards bad habits. This is only what the local plod managed to get out of the widow, who's a bit of a quivering mess apparently, but one of the bobbies called to the scene spotted something the lady had mercifully missed when she took one look at her late husband and ran screaming for help.'

'That being what, precisely?'

'A head wound, hidden by his unruly mop of hair, or so the brief wire said. It's still possible that he died of a heart attack brought on by the shock of that, but that's why I need you there.'

They seemed to arrive at the curate's cottage in no time at all and Carlyle asked Adelaide to do her best to get some sort of coherent story out of the hysterical widow while he accompanied Jennings into the cluttered study, where the late Thomas Enderby was draped, face down in a seated position, across his former desk. On the desk in front of him were a sherry decanter half full of sherry and two glasses, both of which were almost empty.

'Has anyone touched these?' Carlyle demanded.

The constable who was solemnly guarding the corpse shook his head. 'Standard procedure ter touch nuffin', sir.'

'Not even the body?

'No, sir. It's just like it were when I found it. I sent Constable Jenkins ter inform the station, then stayed wi' the body. There's bin nobody but me in 'ere since Mrs Enderby found the poor man.'

'Excellent,' Carlyle whispered as he moved round the back of the desk and leaned forward to examine the gash in the back of the deceased's head, which he matched carefully with the base of the heavy candlestick that lay on the carpet behind the desk. 'Well he wasn't beaten to death, that's for certain,' he observed as he looked back up at Jennings across the table.

'You sure about that?' Jennings asked.

Carlyle gave him the benefit of a long look. 'Familiar with the expression about having a dog and barking oneself, Inspector? You brought me here to investigate a sudden death and I'm telling you that the scalp wound was not the cause of death.'

'I'm just enquiring how you can be certain,' Jennings persisted. 'Call it part of my essential police training in medical matters.'

'Very well,' Carlyle conceded. 'For a start, the weapon is not heavy enough to have caused any serious damage, assuming it to have been the one on the floor there, with bloodstains on it. I won't be able to confirm the absence of skull damage until I get the body down to the hospital mortuary. But secondly and more convincingly, there's very little blood.'

'Well there wouldn't be, would there, if it didn't puncture an artery or something?'

Carlyle sighed. 'Ever cut yourself shaving?'

'Of course.'

'And how much blood did that generate?'

'A lot.'

'Precisely. It's not just arteries that bleed, Inspector. You can generate quite a lot of blood from the veins across the skull, and I'd expect more blood than I'm seeing here if the deceased had been whacked while still alive.'

'Why is that?'

Carlyle stood upright. 'The blood that courses through our veins and arteries is pumped by the heart. Think of it as the body's steam engine. When the heart stops, so does the pumping. So if you find a dead body with very little blood around what might be mistaken for the fatal wound you can be reasonably certain that the victim died before that wound was inflicted. So then you go looking for the actual cause of death, which is almost certainly related to a stoppage of the heart. If you look at our victim's face, it's an unhealthy red colour, tending towards purple. And yet the hands are lily-white and the man worked mainly indoors, out of any browning effect from the elements. His widow also reported that he kept himself fit, so no natural reason for a red face after exertion. The bloom on the face comes from what is popularly called a "heart attack" — in medical terms a "cardio-vascular infarction".'

Jennings was confused and it showed in his face. 'Why would a person whack somebody over the head when they were already dead?'

'Two possible reasons. The first is an uncontrollable hatred of the victim on the part of the murderer. But if that had been the case here then I'd expect the damage to be to the face. The alternative, which I much prefer on this occasion, is that the blow to the head was a very amateur attempt to distract us from the heart attack.'

'Why?'

'To prevent us from investigating what caused that heart attack in an otherwise healthy man in his mid-thirties. I suspect the answer to lie in that sherry decanter, or at least the glass from which he was drinking.'

'Poison?'

'Either that or *very* bad sherry.'

'And you wish to have the decanter taken down to the hospital so that you can analyse what's left of the contents?'

'That and the glasses from which they were drinking, in addition to that candlestick. Clearly the minister had a visitor and hopefully we can learn a little more about that visitor from what Adelaide has been able to find out. But those objects must be taken away carefully. I insist that your men only hold them if they have a handkerchief or something over their hands, then drop them into a bag, or some other carrying container.'

'Why?'

'Because, when we get back to the hospital, I want to try an experiment that's been lurking in the back of my mind for some time. We can only hope that the murderer wasn't wearing gloves.'

'Some sort of fingerprint search?'

'Watch and learn, Inspector, watch and learn. Now let's get the body shipped out of here, shall we, along with those utensils? And I'd be obliged if you'd assign a police photographer to accompany it. Then we'll see what Adelaide's discovered.'

It transpired that Adelaide had discovered quite a lot, despite the still almost hysterical state of the widow, Margery Enderby. Adelaide had insisted that she take a seat at the kitchen table, then drink a cup of very strong tea.

Margery watched as Adelaide carefully spooned the third sugar into the cup and stirred it and her mouth set in revulsion. 'I don't take sugar,' she insisted.

'You do this morning,' Adelaide instructed her in a voice that belonged in a schoolroom. 'It's very good for shock and once you're over that you'll be able to tell me everything you can remember.'

'Are you with the police?' Margery asked.

Adelaide frowned. 'It'll be a cold day in Hell when the police realise how valuable women could be in investigating crime,' she responded bitterly. 'I'm with Dr Carlyle, who's currently in your husband's study, finding out what he can. But we need your assistance as well. Who was the last person in there with him?'

'A lady. A very nice lady, or so I thought,' Margery told her as for a brief moment she forgot to sob and gulp for air. 'A new parishioner, fresh to the area, she told us. She was interested in perhaps helping with our Bible School, since she's a teacher.'

'So she went into the study to talk to your husband?'

'Yes, and he asked me to serve them sherry, so I did. She was sitting in the visitors' chair across the desk when I took the tray in to them and left it on the desk. I could hear them chatting away happily, so I came back into the kitchen here to wash up our breakfast things. I heard her wishing Tom goodbye, so he must still have been alive then. He must have had his heart attack while I was showing the lady out. If only I'd thought to go in, I might have been able to…'

She broke off, sobbing pitifully with her head resting on her extended arms across the table.

Adelaide waited until the third wave had subsided, then asked quietly, 'When you heard the lady leave, did you hear your husband's voice as well?'

'No, but I wouldn't have done, would I, from that distance? He was still behind his desk, I imagine. And if he'd been taken ill while the lady was in there, she'd have called for help, wouldn't she?'

'Yes, quite probably. Do you by any chance remember this lady's name?'

'Only her first name. Mary. I was minded of Mary Magdalene, since she had such a lovely smile.'

'It's just that we may need to speak to her, to see if your husband appeared to be feeling ill before she left.'

'Byfleet,' Margery suddenly remembered. 'Byfleet, or something similar to that.'

'Byfield?'

'Could have been. What will the police do with my husband's body? Only I'll need to organise the funeral.'

'He'll be taken down to the London Hospital, where my father will need to confirm that it was a heart attack that killed him, but I'm sure he'll give that priority, so the body should be brought back sometime tomorrow I imagine.'

'It doesn't seem right to be referring to Tom as "the body",' Margery said as she broke down again.

Adelaide slipped discreetly out of the kitchen to join the rest of them in the study.

'We can try that experiment we were talking about!' Carlyle said excitedly as she appeared in the doorway to the study, where one police officer was gingerly transferring items from his covered hand into a bag being held open by his colleague.

Adelaide looked uncertain for a moment, then the penny dropped as she watched the objects being loaded, presumably prior to being taken away. 'The one with the static prints?'

'The very same. But what did you learn from the widow?'

'His final visitor was a woman, apparently. One who sounded vaguely familiar and who may have been using the name "Byfield". That surely can't be a coincidence.'

'Did she see anything of what happened?' Jennings asked.

Adelaide shook her head. 'Unfortunately not. She served them sherry, then got on with domestic duties in the kitchen. She heard the woman wish the deceased goodbye, then showed her out. When she came back in here to collect the sherry things she found her husband dead. But we can't eliminate the possibility that he was already dead when the "Byfield" woman left.'

'It was no natural heart attack, anyway,' Carlyle confirmed. 'Nor, I strongly suspect, did it have anything to do with the somewhat superficial blow to the back of his head, which you can't see immediately because the deceased was in urgent need of a barber. My suspicion is a poison that brought on a myocardial infarction, but we'll know that once I open him up in the mortuary, which is where we'll be heading once the wagon arrives to cart the body away. I've asked for a police photographer to be in attendance as well.'

'It would make sense for the murderer to have been a woman,' Jennings observed. 'The doctor tells me that the blow to the head wasn't inflicted with any force, which is of course consistent with it having been struck by a woman.'

'There you go, underestimating the power of a woman again,' Adelaide goaded him. 'But this woman is not one to be underestimated, it seems. I'm surprised that you haven't already responded to the revelation that the mysterious visitor who's our number one candidate for the poisoner was using the name "Byfield".'

'I hadn't missed it,' Jennings protested. 'I was about to mention it. "Byfield" was the unmarried name of Mary Miller, was it not?'

'One of them,' Carlyle replied with a smile. 'You may recall that Adelaide and I came to see you at the Yard with some important information before we were coincidentally diverted to this murder scene.'

'Yes — what was it that was so important?'

Carlyle's face beamed in triumph as he supplied the answer. 'Earlier today I consulted the records at the Workhouse from which Mary was adopted and given the family name "Byfield". But before that she had another name entirely and not even "Mary", it would seem.'

'Go on?'

'Before she was adopted, Mary Byfield — or Mary Miller as she's now known — had the birth name of "Bridget Dempsey".'

'It's obviously all beginning to form a pattern,' Jennings agreed as they swayed in the rattling police coach on the short journey from the Stepney vicarage back to the London Hospital. 'The problem is,' he added, 'that I can't quite make out what that pattern is.'

'With your permission,' Carlyle said, 'I'll get the driver to stop outside that art shop in Mile End Road, while I collect a few things.'

Jennings's eyebrows rose enquiringly a few minutes later, as Carlyle climbed back into the coach carrying a blackboard and easel and a paper bag containing a packet of chalks and a small artist's painting brush.

Adelaide caught the look on the Inspector's face and smiled. 'Best not to ask, I've learned. What seems like bizarre behaviour at the time usually turns out to have a purpose to it.'

Back in the mortuary, while they waited for the body to come by separate coach, Carlyle issued a set of instructions to Adelaide. 'First thing is to put the water on for tea. Then, while I get this blackboard and easel set up, pour me a decent measure of that zinc powder into a fresh container, but don't make it up into the normal solution. Just leave it in powder form.'

A few minutes later the tea had been poured and Carlyle stood by the blackboard with a piece of chalk in his hand.

'It's like being back at school,' Adelaide said as she passed over the milk jug to Jennings, 'but I think that we're about to be taught something more interesting than how to write our names.'

'Now then,' Carlyle began, 'we have three names for the lady who seems to have confused us all with her ability to be different people. So let's write each name down in sequence, then underneath each one let's make a note of what she's either done, or is still in the process of doing. We start, logically and chronologically, with "Bridget Dempsey". What do we know about her?'

'She was a child in a Workhouse who got adopted by the Byfields,' Jennings said.

Carlyle nodded as he wrote 'Workhouse adoption by the Byfields', then wrote a second heading of 'Mary Byfield' beneath it and drew a connecting arrow down between them. 'The arrow indicates that at the age of nine she became "Mary Byfield",' he added unnecessarily. 'Now, what have I already missed?'

'That according to Matthew West she made several visits to Artus Skuja before his execution, using the name "Dempsey",' Jennings obliged.

Carlyle made a suitable entry, but with a question mark after it. 'Why did she make those visits and what was her connection with Skuja? We already know part of that, thanks to Matthew. Arson of husband Andrew's pharmacy.'

'And why did "Bridget" become "Mary"?' Adelaide added.

'We know that the Byfields were religious,' Jennings suggested, 'and from what Matthew's brother told us — rather, what his fiancée and Mary's step-sister, told us — that religion was Anglican. "Bridget" is far too Catholic for some tastes and too closely associated with Fenian affiliations, so the choice of "Mary" was probably her parents'. That would be my guess, anyway.'

'And a reasonable conjecture, given that there seems to have been no reason why a child of nine would be adopting an assumed name,' Carlyle agreed. 'There's also the point that this blackboard is getting fairly cluttered already. So we already have Mary Byfield becoming Mary Miller by marrying Andrew Miller and thereby becoming acquainted with Skuja after, and perhaps even before, he set fire to their pharmacy, killed five people and finished up on his way to the gallows. So we now draw an arrow down between the "Byfield" and "Dempsey" entries relating to Skuja and a third heading, "Miller".'

'That's always puzzled me,' Jennings said out loud. 'Why did she carry on using the name "Miller", when it could be traced back to Skuja by way of the fire and why did she volunteer enough information to Matthew to allow us to make the connection?'

'I've had occasion to comment, more than once, Inspector, that if the criminals of this city ever become more intelligent, you and I will find our jobs to be impossible,' Carlyle said. 'She had no idea that Matthew was connected with us and even now she's no idea that Adelaide, who she's met, is my daughter. It was easier for Mary to tell Matthew a half-truth that he wouldn't necessarily disbelieve. It's pure coincidence that Matthew and we are exchanging information.'

'But what's the reason why she made such an effort to cultivate Matthew, to the extent of trying to seduce him?' Adelaide demanded.

Carlyle smiled. 'We don't know that she really *did* try to seduce him, but you're quite right to remind us that she's gone out of her way to get to know him. And, most significantly, to persuade him to stay away from Newgate in future. He was one of those present at Skuja's faked hanging, so she wanted to know how much he knew and also to keep him from investigating further, if that was his intention.'

'But how did she get to know that Matthew had gone investigating?' Jennings asked.

Carlyle nodded. 'A good question, but let's not forget that Matthew had already searched the visitors' book at Newgate. That's how we knew about the visits by "Bridget Dempsey" to Skuja in the first place, if you recall? I would hazard a guess that someone in the prison tipped her off, which brings us round to the unfortunate deaths of those who knew too much, which thankfully hasn't yet included Matthew.'

'And it's to be hoped that it doesn't,' Adelaide muttered as she went pale in the face.

Carlyle raised an eyebrow towards Jennings. 'Is it still your belief that the killings of Skelton, Somerskill, Bryant and Tibbins were all down to Tasker? Given this latest information, could you not perhaps also consider Mary Miller?'

Jennings shook his head. 'Not until Tasker also finishes up dead. Those killings had all the brutal hallmarks of a man.'

Carlyle smiled. 'Or men paid to do the dirty deeds by a woman. And you are presumably aware that poison is a woman's choice of murder weapon, so you cannot, can you, reasonably exclude Mary Miller from responsibility for the murder of Arthur Skelton — Artus Skuja as was — and now Thomas Enderby? Bear in mind, as we have already discussed only recently, that Mary Miller has some familiarity with poisons through her late husband's pharmacy enterprise, and add to that the fact that the last person we know of who saw Enderby alive was a woman whose name and vague description could apply to Mary Miller.'

'But until we can prove — if we ever can — that Miller *was* that visitor, then I'll stick to Tasker as my main suspect.'

'Thereby exposing Matthew to continuing danger?' Adelaide protested.

Jennings shrugged. 'That can't be helped, since he's chosen to ignore my advice and no doubt yours also, to pull his head in.'

'You underestimate his bravery, his loyalty to any cause that he puts his name to, and his downright stubborn nature,' Adelaide complained. 'And have you been following Tasker, as you were intending to do? What, if anything, has he been doing to earn your ongoing suspicion?'

'Nothing, to be perfectly candid,' Jennings admitted. 'My men have been following him assiduously, and I may say racking up all sorts of expenses as they tail him from one low pub to another, but apart from consorting with prostitutes up back alleys, he's done nothing unlawful. He still attends his work every day inside Newgate and we can't follow him inside there, but otherwise he's kept his nose clean.'

'But whoever that woman was who visited Enderby, it clearly can't have been John Tasker,' Carlyle pointed out.

Jennings shrugged again. 'As I already said, you can't prove that the female visitor was Miller and you don't even know that Enderby's heart attack was brought on by poison. If it comes to that, you don't even know that it *was* a heart attack.'

A heavy thump on the mortuary door brought a smile to Carlyle's face. 'Right on cue,' he muttered, as he inclined his head in a signal for Adelaide to open the door.

Two burly constables carried a stretcher into the room and on an instruction from Carlyle they decanted the body onto the slab in the centre. A third man was hanging back in the doorway, loaded down with various items of equipment that Carlyle invited him to leave in a corner of the room once he'd established that he was a police photographer. Then it was Jennings's turn to receive an instruction.

'I assume that you don't wish to be present when I make deep incisions into the corpse of the late Reverend Enderby, so perhaps you might like to accompany your photographer colleague upstairs for a cup of tea in the public cafeteria. Adelaide will come and fetch you when it's appropriate.'

Once they had the mortuary to themselves, Adelaide set about stripping the body and washing it with a thin solution of formalin, to kill any surface germs and to make the room smell a little sweeter once the abdominal cavity was exposed to the air.

In less than a minute the rib cage had been dispensed with and Carlyle gave a sigh of satisfaction. 'As I predicted. The poor man's myocardium was blown apart. She must have used enough to fell an ox. All we need to do now is trace it in the bloodstream and that's your job. I'll sew him back together while you go looking for digitalis.'

Less than an hour after they had begun to savour the delights of the ground floor cafeteria, Inspector Jennings and his photographer colleague were called back down to the mortuary. Carlyle was waiting by the cadaver with a small piece of paper in his hand that he handed to Jennings. 'I wrote out the full medical gobbledegook for you, in order that you can impress them with it at the Yard, but the simple explanation is that the vicar with the head wound died from digitalis poisoning. It makes the heartbeat increase to an alarming level in even a healthy person and eventually the heart blows apart. Think in terms of an exploding boiler on a railway locomotive.'

'Thank you for that,' Jennings acknowledged. 'Can I have the body back? If so, I'll have it conveyed to the widow, who'll never be allowed to learn that her late husband was poisoned by someone who was believed to be a parishioner.'

'And are you yet prepared to believe that it was Mary Miller?' Carlyle asked, causing the obstinate frown to return to the inspector's face.

'I was giving that some thought while having one of the worst cups of tea I've ever tasted. I still have a very basic question in my mind, and that is why would Mary Miller want to get involved in some scheme to save Skuja from the gallows when he was the cause of her husband's death and a possible future blackmailer?'

Carlyle sighed. 'I seem to recall that we've had this conversation before and my response has not altered in any way. First of all, in my experience it's impossible to predicate any form of rationality in criminal behaviour. Secondly, we cannot get totally into the mind of another person. And finally, in this present case, I can think of several reasons. The first is that she was paid handsomely to do it. The second is that she wished to employ Skuja's dubious talents for reasons of her own. The third is that she is mad, which would explain why she later went on to poison him when he became "Skelton". Either that or he pushed his luck too far when he tried to blackmail her.'

Jennings shook his head in exasperation. 'It's all too much for a simple brain like mine. But you haven't proved that she even poisoned Skelton, which is where all this began, remember.'

'If I can prove that she poisoned Enderby,' Carlyle challenged him, 'would you begin to at least consider the possibility that she also murdered Skelton?'

'Then I would be obliged to,' Jennings conceded, 'although it still wouldn't pin all those other deaths on her.'

'Then we must take this step by step. Adelaide has succeeded in detecting a massive dose of digitalis — or, perhaps more appropriately, "foxglove", since she employed a simple reactive process that revealed the presence of the derivative plant.'

'In the decanter that you insisted that we bring back?' Jennings asked.

Carlyle nodded. 'Also in the bloodstream of the deceased and in one of the glasses that we found still on the deceased's desk. Since there was none in the other glass, we may assume, may we not, that this other glass was the one used by Mary Miller?'

'Mary Miller, or whoever the poisoner was,' Jennings conceded.

Carlyle nodded. 'But since we know it was a woman who shared the sherry with the deceased, Adelaide advised me of something back at the vicarage that I would have been in danger of overlooking. Perhaps I should let her explain.'

Adelaide took over the conversation. 'We have reason to believe that Mary Miller likes to consider herself a lady of fashion and breeding. Sherry — which is the drink that was being served by the hospitable vicar who believed that he was meeting a new parishioner who would assist with his Bible School — is not only a light shade of brown, as you will note from what remains in the decanter, but it is also sticky. A fashion-conscious lady of breeding would therefore remove her glove and possibly both of them, before taking the glass in her hand. Do I need to say more, Inspector?'

'You're obviously hinting at some sort of finger impression,' Jennings reasoned out loud, 'but how do you know that one will remain on the glass she used and that you can reveal it?'

It was time for Carlyle to pick up the thread. 'You probably wondered, first of all why I stopped off at the art shop for this brush and secondly why I asked for the attendance of your photographer colleague here, who has so far remained commendably quiet and displayed considerable patience. In a few moments we hope to employ his services. The zinc container please, Adelaide.'

Adelaide brought the zinc and laid it on the side counter, along with the glass believed to have been handled by Mary Miller. Carlyle dipped the paintbrush into the container several times, emerging on each occasion with a quantity of zinc power that he brushed lightly across the glass until he gave a shout of delight and blew the unwanted residue of the zinc powder off it, to form a light cloud of dark grey as it drifted away. There on the glass remained the faint outline of a fingerprint.

Carlyle took the fingerprint impression they had taken from the dead hand of Enderby and held it up alongside the faint image, inviting Jennings to compare the two. 'They are different, are they not?'

'Clearly,' Jennings conceded. 'But how do you intend to make use of this second one?'

'It will not survive for more than an hour or so, by my reckoning,' Carlyle told him, 'so if you would be so good, Mr Photographer, I'd like you to obtain as clear an image as you can of what you see here on the glass, while Adelaide and I see what we can find on the stopper of the decanter.'

Fifteen minutes later they had two photographic negatives inside the camera and the photographer was sent back to the Yard to develop them without delay. Jennings was still looking stunned as Carlyle spelt out the obvious.

'You now have proof that someone other than Thomas Enderby handled not only the other glass during his small but tragic meeting over sherry, but also the stopper from the decanter. It is hardly stretching the chain of reasoning to breaking point to suggest that whoever owns that fingerprint found an opportunity to slip a foxglove extract into the sherry before graciously declining a second glass. The unfortunate host, however, having a weakness for alcohol that has ruined many a fellow cleric over the years, took a second glass that proved fatal.'

'Two things,' Jennings commented, still amazed by what he had just witnessed. 'If that experiment of yours just now proves successful, then we've discovered a new and highly valuable, weapon in our relentless fight against crime. We can go to the scene of every burglary, rape, robbery or murder and look for things that the criminal touched. The jail cells will be full inside a month!'

'Until criminals get wise to it and wear gloves,' Adelaide pointed out.

Carlyle nodded. 'There is also the little matter of persuading juries of the reliability of fingerprint collection and comparison. But what was your second point?'

'The obvious one that you have nothing to compare the offending fingerprint with,' Jennings pointed out. 'You have convincingly demonstrated that the glass and the decanter were handled by a person other than the deceased and you have predicated the means by which the poison could have been introduced into the sherry, but until you can find the owner of that fingerprint, we can go no further. One fingerprint is as useless as the single blade on a pair of scissors.'

'Then we shall have to persuade our favoured suspect to supply that fingerprint for comparison, shall we not?' Carlyle said confidently. 'And Adelaide already has a plan.'

16

'This is very generous of you,' Matthew murmured as he cut into the salmon steak on his supper plate. He was seated round the dining table at the Hackney home of the Carlyles and he was further elated by the fact that Adelaide seemed to be in one of her good moods.

'It's the least we can do,' she assured him with a warm smile, 'after all your hard work on my behalf and your loyal attendance during my many attempts to secure votes. Not that I seem to have attracted too many expressions of support and we're only a few weeks away from the election now.'

'May I make a further suggestion, which I do solely out of loyalty to your cause and without any implied criticism of what you've been telling the electorate so far?' Matthew asked deferentially, hoping that it wouldn't get her back up and plunge her into one of her wildly defensive tirades.

'Of course,' Adelaide agreed. 'One of Father's favourite expressions is that one should not employ a dog then seek to bark oneself. Not that I think of you as a dog!' she added, horrified as she caught the warning look on her father's face. '*Do* please feel free to advise me, since I value your advice as someone who regularly preaches to crowds.'

'Well,' Matthew continued, choosing his words with care, 'up until now your speeches have been about the poverty and deprivation in the East End slums to the south of here. Conditions that I'm only too familiar with, and I can only applaud your noble and inspired desire to do something for the benefit of those who have to live there. But those are not the people who you're relying on to elect you, are they?'

'But they're the people I wish to help,' Adelaide began to bridle. 'Are you about to suggest that I ignore their plight, just like all the other pompous self-satisfied balloons who're seeking election? All male, of course,' she added with evident distaste.

'Let the man finish, Adelaide,' Carlyle advised her quietly.

'Yes, I'm sorry, Matthew,' Adelaide replied. 'Do please continue.'

'Well,' Matthew continued, 'if you want to be elected as a councillor for Hackney, then you need to tell the voters of Hackney what they want to hear. What will persuade them to vote for you. And most of them are male. Regrettable, but true. So you have to ask yourself what the male voters of Hackney want from you, if they're to be persuaded to elect you.'

'And what might that be?'

'Put yourself in the position of those who live here, many of whom have only just arrived since that recent spate of new housing development. Even I can see the changes in the place since I first began visiting you and it must be causing considerable concern for those who've been here for a long time, in addition to those who've moved in from other suburbs hoping to find more fresh air and green spaces, only to see the locality slowly degenerating.'

'But I can hardly expect to gain support if I decry Hackney as a developing slum, can I?' Adelaide argued.

Matthew shook his head. 'Of course not, and that's not what I'm suggesting. What I *am* suggesting is that you make a list of the things that you find most irritating and perhaps unpleasant, about living here, then promise to do something about them.'

'Starting with the state of the streets,' Carlyle suggested. 'Collins is forever complaining about the piles of horse dung he has to steer around and the ever increasing traffic as he tries to get out onto Cambridge Road to take me down to the hospital.'

'A very good start,' Matthew enthused. 'And I've heard several complaints, while you were standing on that street corner near the police station in St Thomas's Road, as I believe it's called, that there seems to have been an alarming increase in the number of burglaries in this area. You need to address more issues like that. Tell the voters how you'll campaign relentlessly to ensure that Hackney is restored to being the respectable green oasis against urban squalor that it used to be.'

'A nice turn of phrase,' Adelaide conceded, 'but won't it make me seem too — too "elitist" or something? I'd be no better than the Tory candidate if I started mouthing sentiments like that.'

'But you believe that people, even here in Hackney, should be able to lead decent, healthy lives, don't you?' her father asked.

Adelaide was forced to concede that she was committed to precisely that sort of thing, then turned back to Matthew. 'Would you be so good as to put some of your thoughts down on paper for me? Including that lovely line about "the respectable green oasis against urban squalor", or however you expressed it just now.'

'Then you might like to think up ways in which that could be brought about without increasing the tax burden on those who live here,' Carlyle added with a wry smile. 'So how shall these fine words be delivered to the populace, do you propose?'

On cue, Adelaide appeared to receive inspiration. 'Let's go back into Victoria Park, and invite along everyone we know! I'll get Constance and Emily to prepare a lovely picnic again and you can write me a really winning speech. You can even invite that dreadful Miller woman along, if you like.'

145

'I thought you'd taken a dislike to her, after you suspected her of trying to seduce me. Wrongly, of course.'

'Whether she sought to seduce you, rightly *or* wrongly, is not why I dislike her,' Adelaide protested. 'I dislike her because I believe her to be a liar and a hypocrite who has neither the intention nor the ability to bring about reform of the death penalty laws. But she did once offer to bring her friends along to support my election campaign.'

'Don't you think you'd be in danger of hypocrisy yourself if you invited her along despite what you think of her?' Matthew asked, to a warning cough and a slight shake of the head from Carlyle.

Adelaide took a deep breath and forced a smile to her face. 'I have no doubt that many of those upon whose support I shall be relying when it comes to the voting will be people whose morals I would despise, but that shouldn't prevent me from seeking their vote, should it?'

'A good point,' Matthew conceded, 'but I'm not sure that I'll be seeing Mrs Miller in the foreseeable future in order to issue the invitation. And since she lives in Islington, I'm not sure how many of her friends would be interested in the immediate future of Hackney.'

'Has she abandoned her plans for a campaign against hanging?' Carlyle asked.

Matthew shrugged. 'I've no idea, since she hasn't been in touch lately. And I must own that my enthusiasm for joining anything with which she's associated has flagged somewhat since I learned of her involvement in that fire that wiped out an entire family.'

'To be fair to her, we don't know that she was involved directly, or knew anything about it,' Adelaide replied, to a warning look from her father.

But Matthew had seized on the point. 'I'm bound to observe that you've changed your position all of a sudden,' he said suspiciously.

Adelaide recovered from her near blunder as she replied, 'You know my stand on the position of women, Matthew, so don't get me started on that again. The fire was no doubt commissioned by her husband and all she could do was stand meekly by and let it happen. And from what Father told me, even he was insistent that the fire not be lit until the family were well out of the rooms above.'

'That's the case,' Carlyle confirmed with an admiring glance at Adelaide.

It fell silent until Adelaide asked, 'Did you tell your brother, by the way, and did he alert his fiancée to what her step-sister had been caught up in?'

'I did indeed, and he inclined to the same opinion as you, namely that whatever the husband had been up to, Mary probably played no part in it. But I think that conclusion had more to do with his feelings for Susan. Do you want me to invite them along to the picnic, by the way?'

'No,' Carlyle and Adelaide said in unison.

Matthew looked askance. 'You're both adamant on that point, it would seem. Are they not socially acceptable enough?'

'That wasn't my reason,' Carlyle replied quickly. 'My reason was that they're not registered to vote in Hackney.'

'And my reason was that they're probably too busy using their valuable weekends making wedding plans,' Adelaide added diplomatically. 'They both work through the week, so their weekends must be precious to them. That's also true for you, Matthew, I appreciate, which makes me even more grateful to you for taking so much time to support my cause.

I'm so glad that I found a champion who's as committed to political reform as myself.'

As Matthew took his leave later that evening, Adelaide escorted him to the street door and planted a kiss on his cheek as she bid him good night. 'And don't forget to invite that dreadful Miller woman,' she reminded him as he walked down the front path to where Collins had been instructed to draw up the coach. 'A week on Sunday, Victoria Park, 2pm.'

Adelaide walked back into the house, where she found her father smoking a cigar in his study.

'Do you think it worked?' he asked.

Adelaide nodded. 'And I'm getting to like him more every day, even though in some ways he's not fit to be let out without a responsible adult. And I must admit that I have to bite my tongue and clench my teeth when I think that Mary Miller might well get him first. What should that tell me?'

'It should tell you that the sooner we have the woman locked up the better,' Carlyle said. 'Let's hope that Matthew unwittingly plays his part and that your two terrifying friends can achieve what we have planned for them.'

17

'The Trustees were far from impressed that you turned down their virtual free gift of the living in West Ham,' Superintendent Livingstone told Matthew sourly as he stood behind him at the notice board. 'So if your reason for consulting that is to find out what other openings are available, I'd advise against it. For another two years at least, I'd say.'

Matthew sighed and turned round to explain. 'I'm just so busy with other things at the moment, Superintendent. My brother's getting married in June and I'm committed to this campaign to abolish capital punishment.'

'How's that going, as a matter of interest?'

'It's not, at the moment. Mrs Miller hasn't been in touch for a week or two now and I fear that she may have dropped me off her list of potential contributors.'

'We can't have that,' Livingstone insisted. 'If we're not invited, then no doubt the Anglicans will stick their noses in. Or, God help us, the Catholics. Why don't I send her an invitation to come down here and join us for tea one morning, or something along those lines?'

'That would be very helpful,' Matthew said. 'And I need to invite her to something else as well. A friend of mine is standing for election for the LCC and I'm lending a hand in the election campaign. We're hopeful that Mrs Miller can drum up some support.'

'What's his name, this friend of yours?'

'It's actually a woman. You met her that day when she came in with an urgent need for me to accompany her to the

London Hospital, where her father's a surgeon specialising in anatomising the dead. Her name's Adelaide Carlyle.'

'A woman standing for election to the LCC?' Livingstone queried disbelievingly. 'It's unheard of, surely?'

'Yes, which is why she needs all the support she can get. Her ideas are as radical as her determination to break down the male barriers.'

Livingstone frowned. 'Perhaps as well that you declined to take up the living in West Ham, by the sound of it. We don't need to get a reputation for radicalism.'

But the superintendent's promise was fulfilled three days later when Matthew returned from conducting his thrice-weekly Bible class to find Mary Miller sitting in the private consultation room that by unspoken agreement had become his own personal office.

'I hope you don't mind,' she cooed as she planted another instalment of lipstick on his cheek, 'but I received this lovely letter from your superintendent, advising me that you'd passed over a recent promotion in order to work more closely with me and that you were wondering what progress had been made towards our plans to lobby Parliament. I'm here to invite you to write our provisional manifesto.'

'I'm very flattered,' Matthew replied truthfully. 'When would you require it by?'

'Whenever is most convenient for you,' Mary replied. 'I must own that it has proved difficult to get everyone committed to a day on which we can all meet together in the one place, so I've taken to speaking to you individually. We could perhaps arrange for you to call on me for afternoon tea again when you have the first draft ready? I was sorting out some of my old chests the other day and I found some of my old catalogues. You know, the ones I mentioned to you at our last meeting, when I was modelling our range of undergarments? You might find it amusing, as one who promotes modesty in all things, to see how some women used to disport themselves.'

'Actually,' Matthew replied as he tried not to blush, 'I also have something to invite you to. You remember my friend Adelaide Carlyle, who's hoping to be elected to the LCC? Well on one occasion when you and she met, you very graciously undertook to interest some of your friends in her cause. We're planning a public meeting at Speakers' Corner in Victoria Park on the Sunday after next — the twenty-sixth — and if I might hold you to that promise, then perhaps I could see my way clear to bringing my manuscript over to your house the following week. Then I could also admire your catalogues.'

'Splendid!' Mary enthused. 'So let me make a note of that date. Sunday 26th, wasn't it?' she asked as she reached into her bag for her notebook and pencil and began writing. 'Somewhere in a park, you said?'

'Victoria Park, in Hackney,' Matthew confirmed. 'At one of the places they call "Speaker's Corner". Use the Hackney Gate, then turn off to the left and head for the Burdett-Coutts Fountain. It's just down towards the boating pond from there.'

Mary took her leave, still gushing at the prospect of Matthew paying her a visit at home and Matthew chuckled to himself once he was alone again. Perhaps Adelaide was right and Mary did have his seduction on her agenda. He would of course politely resist, but Adelaide perhaps only had herself to blame. And perhaps he could learn more about why Mary had lied to him about the reason for her late husband's suicide. He owed that much to Charles and Susan.

18

There was a much larger crowd at Victoria Park this time, possibly because the LCC elections were only three weeks away, and Matthew smiled with satisfaction as he saw Mary Miller approaching their picnic spot under the tree, accompanied by three other women who were presumably influential friends of hers. He sidled up to Adelaide, who had her head down in the written notes that Matthew had left with her several days previously.

'Looks like Mary Miller kept her promise — and she has some friends with her.'

'Excellent!' Adelaide replied with a smile. 'Which is more than can be said for your writing. There are some words here I can only guess at. Are clergymen trained in the same school as doctors in how to scribble down things in such a way as to be indecipherable?'

'Make up the bits you can't read,' he replied. 'I have to go and welcome Mary on your behalf.'

Adelaide frowned as she asked, 'Are you sure it's not on your own behalf?'

'That too, I suppose,' Matthew conceded.

'Make sure that Constance and Emily invite her to share the picnic,' Adelaide instructed him, 'then get back over here and introduce me to the crowd, before they get bored and walk away.'

A broad smile lit up Mary Miller's face as Matthew walked towards her. She scurried towards him over the uneven grass, leaned forward and planted a very visible lipstick bow on his cheek, then indicated her companions. 'I kept my part of the bargain, lovely man. Now make sure that you keep yours — shall we say Tuesday coming, at 3pm?'

'I have instructions to invite you to partake of the picnic over there,' Matthew nodded and smiled as he led her gently by the arm towards the spread blanket, the opened hamper and the various goodies already being consumed. As also instructed by Adelaide, and reminded of several times during the past hour, he beckoned to Constance Wilberforce and she rose to her feet and came towards them with remarkable speed.

'This is Mary Miller,' he told Constance, who smiled more widely than he had ever seen her do and took Mary gently by the arm.

'We are *so* honoured to have you with us today,' she gushed, as she nodded towards Emily Peveril, who rose to her feet and gave a magnificent impression of a genteel lady who'd already had too much wine for a hot day.

'Pleeshed to meet you,' she minced as she swayed slightly, holding out a bottle of indeterminate contents. 'Thish cherry brandy'sh splendid, but it tendsh to stain the clothing, I'm afraid.' She looked down at a red stain on the collar of her light yellow costume, hiccupped and giggled.

'Do please forgive my dear friend Emily,' Constance said in a tone of moderate embarrassment, 'but her constitution is not that of a person accustomed to strong alcoholic beverages. She's right about the liqueur, though — would you care for a glass?'

'Not just at the moment,' Mary replied slightly disdainfully, adding, 'Not on an empty stomach, anyway,' as she nodded suggestively towards the open hamper.

'Easily solved,' Constance said. 'We've only just unpacked the hamper and you simply *must* try one of these chicken drumsticks before they disappear. Allow me,' she offered before Mary could protest and a moment later she bustled back holding a chicken drumstick carefully between two fingers. 'They were marinated in claret before they were cooked and I've had two already,' she told Mary. 'They're delicious — do please try one.'

With a polite smile, Mary unfastened her gloves and placed them carefully in the pocket of her costume jacket, then reached out and took the chicken leg. She took a delicate bite. 'Delicious indeed,' she murmured as she took several more bites, then looked around for somewhere to place the bone.

Constance had briefly gone back to the hamper and returned with a glass of the cherry brandy that Emily had been recommending, holding it carefully by its stem. 'You might want to moisten your palate before you try one of the salmon sandwiches,' she suggested.

Mary took the glass from her and tried a sip. Then she screwed up her face slightly and handed it back. 'Not quite to my taste, I'm afraid,' she explained. 'Do you by any chance have anything white?'

Constance scuttled off back to the hamper, giving Emily a sly wink as she passed her. Emily then rose to her feet and began singing 'The Lights of London' in a wavering soprano voice before falling back heavily on to the grass and giggling loudly.

Matthew had been watching this in total amazement and not a little embarrassment. He'd gone to the trouble of inviting Mary as requested and she must have formed the most dismal impression of Adelaide's friends, particularly the normally demure Emily. He watched Mary being invited to take a seat on the blanket, then became conscious of Adelaide at his elbow and turned with the intention of registering his opinion of her friend, then thought twice about it when he saw the broad smile on her face.

'What are you grinning at?' he asked, bemused. 'Your dear friend Emily just disgraced herself in front of our invited guest!'

'You noticed, did you?' she chuckled gleefully.

Matthew couldn't believe it. 'Of *course* I noticed, as no doubt did the lady you particularly asked me to invite.'

'I hope so,' Adelaide said, 'then she wouldn't have paid any attention to what Connie was up to. Anyway, time for my ringmaster to open the circus — up you go.'

Matthew stepped onto the concrete plinth reserved for speakers, took a deep breath and began his opening address. 'Ladies and gentlemen, thank you for your attention at this important time for London's immediate future. We are only three weeks away from the forthcoming LCC elections and you have no doubt been recently bombarded with solicitations from candidates who are seeking your vote, to the point at which you are confused as to where to place your cross on the ballot paper. Well, I bring good news, because I can put an end to that confusion. There is only one obvious candidate for Hackney, if you wish to see this wonderful borough continue to bloom in splendour as a perfect location to bring up your family. She has, unlike her rivals for election, lived all her life here in Hackney and has its best interests dearly in her heart. I give you Miss Adelaide Carlyle.'

Adelaide shook Matthew's hand for the benefit of the onlookers, then raised her pencil thin skirt modestly in order to step up and replace him on the concrete square. Almost before the spattering of applause had died down she had begun, opening with an impromptu line that wasn't on the pencilled notes that Matthew had prepared for her.

'Thank you, as ever, to Matthew West, a dedicated man of God whose selfless ministry in the East End at Shadwell has made him only too familiar with what can happen to an area when overcrowding, squalor, dirt and the indifference of the authorities combine to render it a slum. I am totally committed to preventing that from happening here in my home suburb of Hackney, a beautiful green lung on the outskirts of some of the worst hovels in this great city of ours. You, like my parents, moved here in order to afford our families a better life, but already we see the signs of neglect creeping north out of Bethnal Green and Spitalfields. The increase in street traffic, with its accompanying soil from horses, the tolerance of new and cluttered housing developments by a council whose only concern is to ensure that their well-heeled friends get the contracts. And the failure to allocate enough police to the district in order to stem the increasing crime that this previously peaceful spot has attracted. I shall make it my first priority to ensure that those who have enjoyed power within local government for far too long are reminded of the duty they owe to its loyal, but long-suffering, residents.'

It went on in the this vein for another ten minutes and Adelaide eventually stepped down to enthusiastic applause and several shouts of encouragement from the crowd that had grown to over a hundred. She walked back proudly to where Matthew had been joined by Mary Miller, hanging on his arm and beaming her appreciation.

'A magnificent speech, my dear,' Mary murmured condescendingly. 'I shall see to it that as many of my friends as possible vote for you on the all-important day. Did you write all that yourself, or may I assume that you had some assistance from this excellent young wordsmith here?' she asked as she snuggled up to Matthew.

Adelaide gave her the benefit of what looked like a genuine smile and thanked her for her kind words. Mary then announced that she had to be leaving and Adelaide asked if she had enjoyed the picnic.

'Indeed I did, my dear, but I should caution you against taking too much of that rather overdone cherry brandy. As you no doubt witnessed, it had quite an unfortunate effect on your young friend over there.'

With that she breezed off, after planting another lipstick ring on Matthew's cheek.

Adelaide allowed Mary to move out of her hearing before she took out her handkerchief and wiped off the lipstick mark with a chuckle. 'The effect that the cherry brandy had on Emily's nothing compared with the consequences it'll have for that two-faced cow.'

19

There was an atmosphere of tense excitement between father and daughter as Carlyle led Adelaide down the dimly lit basement corridor and unlocked the mortuary door. Then he lit the several gas lamps that would provide the light that they needed, while Adelaide opened the jar containing the zinc powder and with a slightly trembling hand poured a generous portion into a container and extracted the brush from the drawer in the office.

It was well after eight in the evening, but they had been too excited to wait when Adelaide returned from her successful address to the voters of Hackney bearing her trophy, carefully wrapped in the napkin that Constance had sealed it in during the picnic. If the plan had worked, they now had a perfect imprint of Mary's greasy fingers on the side of the glass.

Fifteen minutes later, Carlyle gave a grunt of satisfaction as he surveyed the collection of ridges and whorls highlighted in dark grey on the side of the glass, while Adelaide gave a whoop of delight.

'We've got her!' she exclaimed, but her father was a little less elated.

'We have, provided that this lasts until the morning.'

'Doesn't Scotland Yard work through the night?' she asked.

'No doubt it does, but not that part of it that we need. I'll just nip upstairs and borrow the telephone in the administration office in order to leave an urgent message for Inspector Jennings when he arrives for work tomorrow morning. Then I think we should head home with this valuable addition to my researches carefully preserved under one of those bell jars to keep it from the air. Also the less motion to which we subject it the better.'

'Is that all it is to you, Father?' Adelaide asked. 'Just an addition to your experiments with finger impressions? Surely, armed with this we can prove that it was Mary Miller who killed the Reverend Enderby?'

Carlyle gave her a quizzical smile. 'And also put her away where she can't seduce Matthew?'

'That also,' Adelaide conceded, 'but didn't Jennings say that if this works he can virtually put an end to crime in London?'

'Yes, he did, which I fear may have been a somewhat optimistic assertion. But it will certainly help, to begin with at least. And both you and he are overlooking the point that the courts have to be persuaded that there's some value in comparing finger impressions. Some scientific validity, that is. In order to achieve that, we need to collect thousands more of them and prove that we have never found two the same.'

'But surely,' Adelaide continued to argue, 'if we can show that the fingerprint on the glass that we know is Mary Miller's is the same as the one we found on the glass and decanter in Enderby's study the day someone administered digitalis to him, we've raised a very strong suspicion that it was her?'

'A "strong suspicion", certainly, but is that enough to prove her guilt "beyond reasonable doubt", which is the standard employed by juries? What the fingerprint comparison gives us is what they call "circumstantial evidence". What that means is evidence that points strongly to her guilt. There is always the possibility that some smart defence counsel gifted with scientific skills, like that tricky Mr Marshall Hall whose name seems to dominate every criminal trial report these days, will succeed in bamboozling the jury with pseudo-scientific mumbo jumbo that sounds impressive, but is in fact utter rubbish. We need something more than the fingerprint comparison before we can guarantee that Mary Miller will hang for the murder of the Reverend Enderby.'

'Would it be enough to justify Jennings arresting her?' Adelaide asked as she began to formulate another scheme.

'Probably,' Carlyle agreed, 'but is that all *you're* interested in, while you criticise me for my concentration on expanding medical jurisprudence — are you just anxious for Mary Miller to be taken out of Matthew's way?'

'You should have seen how the cheap hussy was making up to him in the park earlier today,' Adelaide hissed. 'I just wanted to ram one of Constance's cream sponge fingers up her painted nose, but instead I had to be nice to her!'

'If you don't want another woman to get their hands on Matthew, then you'd better claim him for yourself, before he goes off the boil.'

'*What* boil? I haven't seen any evidence of him getting all hot under the collar for me,' Adelaide argued.

Carlyle smiled. 'No wonder, since you keep him at arms' length and make it very clear that any amorous advance will lead to him receiving his marching orders. You *must* let him inside your guard, to employ a boxing term.'

'But he's a man!' Adelaide objected.

Carlyle chuckled. 'It's to be hoped so.'

'Ugh!' Adelaide responded instinctively, then returned to her original question regarding the strength of the evidence they already had against Mary. 'If she's arrested, they'd be authorised to take a photograph of her, would they not?'

'So I understand,' Carlyle confirmed, 'but so what?'

'And if the Enderby widow were to confirm, when shown that photograph, that Mary Miller was the lady who visited her husband just before he had his heart attack, would that help?'

'Of course it would. It would prove that Mary Miller was the last person in Enderby's company before he died. If we combine that with the fact that she had her hand on the decanter and glass just before that death and that the decanter contained digitalis, which was found in the bloodstream of the deceased, who expired as the result of an over-active heart probably stimulated by digitalis, then we almost have her in the net.'

'Why "almost"?' Adelaide countered. 'Surely that's enough?'

'If I were Marshall Hall, or another of those slimy defence lawyers, I'd leave the suggestion with the jury that it was Mrs Enderby who wanted her husband dead. That *she* supplied the sherry by bringing it into the room after lacing it with foxglove extract.'

'Then why did Mary Miller not also die?' Adelaide demanded.

Carlyle looked at her. 'You really are determined to see Mary Miller swing, are you not? I take it that you intend to show the widow a photograph of Mary Miller, assuming that Scotland Yard take one?'

'You can rely on it,' Adelaide said. 'But how do we prove that she murdered Skelton as well as Enderby?'

'By inviting the jury to conclude, once we demonstrate her familiarity with digitalis, that she must have used the same technique with him. But there's a huge legal conundrum there, is there not?'

'What's that?'

'Once we demonstrate that Skelton was Skuja, we are inviting a court to find Mary Miller guilty of murdering someone who was officially dead.'

'I hadn't thought of that. But do we think that she was also behind the murders of the others? Dr Somerskill, Percy Bryant and Sam Tibbins?'

161

'She almost certainly was, and Jennings may be right when he suspects John Tasker's hand to have been in those. Perhaps, when we have Mary Miller safely locked away and facing the hangman, she might be obliging enough to tell us, perhaps in order to preserve her neck from the noose.'

'But she'd still be locked safely away for years?'

'Of course. Certainly long enough for even you to allow Matthew to get close enough inside your guard to show his true feelings. But it's growing late and I for one would welcome an early night ahead of an exciting day tomorrow. Let's finish up here and get Collins to take us home.'

20

'I've not even had time for a cup of tea yet,' Jennings complained as Carlyle and Adelaide were shown into his office at the Yard, Carlyle carrying a tightly wrapped bundle carefully in both hands. 'I got the message as soon as I got in, but it's only 8am for God's sake — have you people had any breakfast?'

'Too excited to eat — either of us,' Carlyle explained as he laid the bell jar carefully down on the desk and equally carefully unwrapped it to reveal the liqueur glass. 'We can all take advantage of your tea room once you've arranged for a photographer to record this in as large a detail as he can.'

'I'm not hungry enough to want to sit in a room full of young men ogling me, as happened last time,' Adelaide announced. 'So I'll just stay here while the photographer does what he has to do. You can bring me a cup of tea when you return, however.'

By the time that her father and Jennings returned with her tea the photographer had been and gone and Adelaide was idly turning over the sheets that had come in over the early morning wire and were now lying on Jennings's desk, relaying details of the previous night's misdeeds to every detective officer in the Yard.

'Those are confidential,' Jennings announced sternly as he reached over her shoulder and closed the folder. 'Did my man take the photographs you wanted?'

'He did,' Adelaide sniffed, 'although he seemed to give greater priority to asking whether or not I was interested in having my photograph taken. And the way he was looking at me, I'm not sure that he had in mind my wearing too many clothes when he did so. But he did get around to telling me that he'd have the results available before dinner time. Or "luncheon", as he called it and he invited me to partake of that with him, as well.'

'The price of beauty,' Jennings smirked. 'But I suggest that we meet back here at, say, two pm, when I should have the second photograph for comparison with the first.'

'You still have it?' Carlyle asked.

Jennings nodded. 'Securely under lock and key, in my desk drawer there. I've even had it mounted on a card, so we can mount the second one under it in order to make the necessary comparisons.'

'And if they match?' Adelaide asked.

'If they match, then we have grounds for arresting Mary Miller,' Jennings said.

'Today?'

'No, best left until tomorrow, when I can organise an arrest team and the necessary paddy wagon. I also need to ascertain the lady's current address.'

'You should have asked Matthew,' Adelaide muttered, 'since he seems to be a welcome caller there. It's in Islington somewhere, if that helps.'

Matthew was certainly a welcome caller the following afternoon, as Gladys led him up the staircase to the door of Mary's suite of rooms and invited him to go through to the sitting room, where 'the Mistress' was waiting for him. Her perfume was almost overpowering as Matthew leaned in for the customary lipstick smear and tactfully pulled his hand from Mary's warm and slightly moist grasp in order to extract a sheaf of papers from the inside pocket of his jacket, then take the seat indicated opposite Mary's as Gladys served the tea without being bidden to do so.

Mary saw Matthew glancing at the pastries in the dish. 'I remembered that you don't like over-sweet things, so I bought in some coconut macaroons. I hope they'll be to your liking and do please help yourself before you read me what you've written by way of our manifesto. While you do so, you might also want to glance through these. Pardon my vanity, but I find it so thrilling to be able to show a handsome man like you what I used to look like in my prime.'

She reached under a sofa cushion and handed Matthew a collection of a dozen or so catalogues for ladies' undergarments 'From the House of Tulip'. Matthew flicked through them out of interest, since his familiarity with what women wore under their outer garments was of approximately the same order as his understanding of the inscriptions on ancient Egyptian tombs. He was just feeling sorry for the women who had to wear such restrictive combinations of lace, whalebone, laces and pins when Mary reminded him that he had yet to sample the macaroons and he reached absent-mindedly for one and bit into it. It tasted rather nice, so he put down the catalogue he'd been perusing in order to take a sip of tea, then indulged himself in eating the remainder of the macaroon and looked back across at Mary, who was grinning.

'Rather "racy", are they not?' she asked.

Matthew nodded. 'I must admit that, as an unmarried clergyman, such things are foreign to my eyes.'

'They're almost ten years old now,' Mary explained, 'and since my figure expanded somewhat under the pleasures of a settled married life I doubt that I could squeeze into those sizes any more. But fashions have changed also, under the influence of our dear Queen as she also expanded in her widowhood, and now the drawers are shorter, more functional and less encumbered with lace. Likewise the corsets, which are more flexible and in many cases without that horrible whalebone that so restricted one's movements. We manufacture only the most recent in our workshop around the corner, although I'm still looking for the ideal model for them. Perhaps Miss Carlyle, if she doesn't succeed in her political ambitions? She's tall, with that "willowy" look that's so "in" at the moment and she'd be ideal. *Do* feel free to help yourself to macaroons.'

Matthew smiled stupidly at the thought of asking Adelaide if she wanted to pose in her undergarments for a catalogue aimed at selling Mary Miller's products, then checked himself as he realised that he was behaving like someone who'd had too many of the brown ales that Charles enjoyed so much at Christmas and other celebrations. He looked back at Mary, intent on offering to go through the manifesto that he'd spent several evenings composing, then blinked in order to bring his vision of her back into clarity.

In order to buy himself time in which to remember what it was he intended to say he bit into another macaroon and heard Mary excusing herself from the room, although her voice seemed distant. Perhaps that was because she was leaving the room he thought, as he took another sip of tea, then leaned back in the armchair as he began to feel the room revolving slightly. Then he came bolt upright as the sitting room door reopened and Mary flounced in, wearing only a pair of drawers and some sort of corset from the top of which her ample bosoms seemed to be waging a battle for release. He was about to protest when she raised a hand to command his silence.

'This is what you foreswore when you declined the cake on your last visit. It would have put you more in the mood for what you see now and we could have transported ourselves to Heaven as we fell upon each other in our frenzy.'

Matthew was struggling for the words that would convey his request that she put her outer garments back on and his eyes were lolling in his head, just as he realised to his horror that she was in the process of unfastening the clips on the corset. Then he was startled back into full consciousness when the door was booted open without warning and there stood Inspector Jennings and two uniform constables.

And behind them stood a spellbound Carlyle and a horrified looking Adelaide.

'Mary Florence Miller, you're under arrest on suspicion of the murder of Thomas Enderby,' Matthew heard Jennings intone as he took in the horrible enormity of the scene that must be presenting itself to Adelaide's eyes. Mary herself seemed to be drawing attention to it as she squealed in alarm and embarrassment and tried to conceal herself behind the heavy drapes that hung on either side of the large display window, pursued by two uniformed bobbies who brought her back out, protesting about her need to preserve her modesty as they employed the wrist restraints while making offensive remarks regarding her exposed undergarments and what might lie beneath them.

'You obviously weren't concerned about your modesty immediately before we arrived,' Adelaide pointed out in loud and icy tones.

Matthew looked up from where he was seated and shook his head, making the room go round on another circuit in front of his eyes. He began to rise to his feet in protest, but felt the entire room reeling more wildly than before and fell back into the chair.

Carlyle stepped forward and looked curiously down at Matthew as he raised two fingers in front of his face and asked, 'How many fingers am I holding up?'

'No idea,' Matthew responded, before turning his face to the side, leaning over the arm of the chair and vomiting onto the carpet.

'I thought as much,' Carlyle said out loud, then turned to Jennings. 'Assuming that the coach you arrived in will have one extra passenger on its return to the Yard, and that victim and prisoner should not be allowed to travel together, could you call for another wagon to transport Mr West down to the London Hospital?'

'Why should he be afforded that courtesy?' Adelaide demanded hotly. 'Why should he not be left to walk home with his tail firmly between his legs, in total disgrace and humiliation?'

'Because I very much doubt his ability to walk at this precise moment,' Carlyle announced. 'Unless I'm seriously mistaken, he's been drugged. Probably morphine or laudanum.' He turned back to speak to Jennings. 'Could you get some men to search the house, Inspector? I believe that when you do you'll find some sort of crude laboratory in here.'

'The room at the back,' Mary told them through clenched teeth. 'And see to it that you don't make a mess.'

Jennings grudgingly allowed Mary to climb into some outer clothing before she was led towards the stairs past a startled looking Gladys standing in the doorway. 'Your mistress will be away for a while,' Jennings told her sarcastically as he passed her. 'Probably upwards of twenty years and perhaps even permanently. You might want to look for another position — and choose your employer more carefully next time.'

In the meantime Carlyle had been conducting rudimentary tests on Matthew, occasionally slapping him across the face to keep him awake, along with stern instructions to 'stay with me, if you want to witness another sunrise,' while Adelaide stood fuming silently in the corner of the room furthest away from the vomit.

'I'll meet you back down in the coach,' she finally announced grumpily as she made her way out of the sitting room and Matthew tried to follow her departure with eyes that were not quite focused enough even to keep Carlyle in sharp perspective.

'It wasn't how it seemed,' he mumbled.

Carlyle grinned. 'A pity you were unconscious for the best bit, when she tried to hide behind the curtain.'

'Was she going to seduce me?' Matthew asked sleepily.

Carlyle shook his head. 'In your condition? Hardly — more likely someone was close by, on hand to take some very interesting photographs for blackmail purposes. Anyway, you're going to be kept under observation in the hospital at least overnight.'

'What will Adelaide think?' was Matthew's next question.

'When she's finished conducting the tests I'll make sure that she gives you the apology you're due. But in fairness to her, it did look very suspicious. And Mary Miller is a very well-endowed lady.'

Two hours later enough blood had been extracted from Matthew's arm for the obvious tests to be conducted down in the mortuary and Adelaide looked up with a frown as she announced, 'Morphine, as you suspected.'

Carlyle nodded. 'Biscuits or tea?'

'Biscuits. Presumably she was careful not to eat one herself.'

'I imagine that the police will have found opium in its raw form in that room of hers,' Carlyle observed. 'She must be quite an accomplished apothecary, but she presumably learned her skills with mortar and pestle while working alongside her husband.'

'But why would she need to drug Matthew in order to seduce him?'

'What makes you think that was her intention?'

'Well, you saw the state of undress she was in when Inspector Jennings forced the door. I can only assume that she was hoping to persuade Matthew to take her to bed.'

'Just out of interest, do you think he would have done, had we not broken in when we did?' Carlyle asked.

Adelaide shook her head. 'That has me a little puzzled, I must admit. I obviously don't know how these things work, but is a man more likely to fall for a woman's wiles when he's drugged?'

'That rather depends on the drug. But I can assure you that if Mary's intentions were to overcome Matthew's natural modesty and innocence, then she made a poor choice of drug. Morphine's what we use to put patients to sleep before operating on them, as you well know.'

'That's what was puzzling me.'

'I'm almost certain that her objective was to render him unconscious so that she could pose with him in compromising tableaux that someone would then come into the room and photograph. Then those photographs would have been used to blackmail Matthew, or to compromise him in some way. In either case, to prevent him pushing any further with enquiries into what transpired on the day that Skuja escaped the gallows.'

'What you're telling me gives me some hope,' Adelaide said. 'If Mary Miller felt that Matthew needed to be unconscious for those photographs, that must mean that she either knew from experience that he wouldn't be a willing participant in a normal seduction, or strongly suspected that he wouldn't. I really do owe him an apology, don't I?'

'You most certainly do. As it happens I'm due to make my four hourly check on him, so you can accompany me for that purpose. I believe that he'll be fit enough to go home tomorrow and Jennings assured me that he'd send someone to his home with reassuring tidings regarding his whereabouts.'

Carlyle led the way to Matthew's bedside, while Adelaide hung back, a shamefaced look giving away her discomfort. Matthew accurately read her body language and grinned back up cheekily. 'Don't think I wouldn't have done, had she not given me the wrong drug.'

'Don't be disgusting!' Adelaide replied testily. 'I was here to offer you a sincere apology for thinking the worst of you, but if you're going to adopt that salacious tone, then I don't think I'll bother.'

'Apology accepted, whether you actually forced the words out of your mouth or not. But she was very anxious for me to eat a cake that she claimed to have baked the last time I was there, so I think she must have tried the same trick before. Was she trying to kill me?' he asked Carlyle, who shook his head.

'I very much doubt it. More likely her agenda was one of blackmail. However, thanks to your experience we can now link her with the illicit preparation of drugs in her second bedroom, so she'll almost certainly pay the price for doing away with poor old Reverend Enderby.'

'However,' Adelaide added, 'in order to tighten the net completely we need to get his widow to identify her from a photograph we have. I had originally intended to take you with me, given your talent for charming the ladies, but now that you've been laid low —'

'I thought I was getting out tomorrow,' Matthew broke in with a meaningful look at Carlyle, who conducted various tests before nodding.

'You're free to go as soon as the day shift comes on in the morning and Sister can sign off on your discharge papers. I'll leave the authorisation at the nurses' station before I leave today.'

'I'll come up and collect you with the coach,' Adelaide offered, 'then we can go down to Stepney together.'

'I really *must* be rehabilitated,' Matthew said, 'but I need to go home and get a fresh set of clothes. I'll also no doubt have to explain myself to my mother.'

'Back to your usual role, under your mother's thumb,' Adelaide teased him. 'I think I preferred the drug-soaked rake who we found in the company of a half-naked woman. And before you make another disgusting comment, that was nowhere near being an offer on my part.'

With that she slipped from his bedside. Carlyle hung back, glanced slyly after her retreating figure until he saw the heavy rubber double doors to the ward closing after her passage through them, then turned back and looked down at Matthew. 'If it's any consolation, young man, I think you may be winning.'

21

'They said you were in hospital,' Alice West called from the head of the staircase, her face expressing her anxiety as Matthew ushered Adelaide through the front door. 'Were you injured, and are you all right now?'

'No and yes, in that order,' Matthew grinned up at her as he gestured for Adelaide to proceed him up the stairs. 'But I have to go out again, once I get a change of clothes. May Miss Carlyle wait for me in the sitting room, and would you be so good as to make her a cup of tea?'

'The tea will be the easy bit,' Alice replied glumly. 'The hard part will be trying to get a civilised word out of your brother. He's been sitting in there all morning with a face like a wet week in Southend, and he refused any breakfast.'

'Things must be bad,' Matthew said. 'We'll pop in and see if we can lift his spirits.'

If anything, Alice West had been underestimating the depth of Charles's gloom as he lifted his eyes only half-heartedly when Matthew and Adelaide joined him in the sitting room. 'Cheer up, baby brother,' Matthew breezed. 'It may not happen.'

'Indeed it may not,' Charles agreed grumpily. 'You damned church types are such sticklers for protocol. It's as if Susan and I are being condemned to live in sin.'

'That may be better than living in Clerkenwell,' Matthew jested, 'but what exactly have we "damned church types" done to dampen your wedding plans?'

'Well, first of all, the local vicar here at St James's won't agree to marry us because we're not regular members of his congregation. He won't even agree to put up the banns because we won't be getting married in his church. Then the vicar of Susan's local church said much the same thing, since I don't even live within his parish. We've been getting the run around everywhere we go and even if we apply for what they call a "common licence" which does away with the need for the banns to be published, we still don't have a church, because Susan's refusing point blank to get married in what she calls "that horrible sanctuary for down and outs in Shadwell". I assume she's referring to your place of employment.'

Matthew frowned. 'She wouldn't be so high and mighty if she was one of those who have a genuine need for what we do down there. You're right about common licences, since we regularly have to apply for them for the "down and outs" who're trying to lead decent Christian lives. As for finding you a church, I've already explained my difficulty in that regard.'

'Thanks for nothing,' Charles muttered as his chin fell back onto his chest.

It was Adelaide's turn to try to cheer him up. 'Have you actually found a church that you'd like? If so, can't Matthew apply for one of these special licences, so that you can get married there?'

'It's not that simple,' Matthew explained. 'The application has to be counter-signed by the minister who's prepared to conduct the service. Which obviously can't be me, for reasons I've already supplied. Anyway, leave it with me, Charles, and I'll see what I can do. If all else fails, I think I may be able to do you a deal in West Ham.'

'Don't exert yourself unduly in that regard,' Charles told him glumly. 'Susan probably won't agree to that either. To be perfectly frank with you both, I think she may be having second thoughts about marrying me at all. She seems to be coming up with objections to everything I try to suggest.'

'Young women often get nervous as their wedding approaches,' Adelaide said by way of reassurance. 'I'm sure that Matthew will come up with something, so keep your spirits up.'

'I never thought of my older brother as a miracle worker,' Charles replied, 'but thanks for trying to cheer me up. What brings you here anyway?'

'I'm here for a change of clothes, then we're off to St Dunstan's, in Stepney,' Matthew told him.

'Thinking of getting married yourselves?' Charles asked. 'If so, perhaps we could make it a double one.'

'How did you come to be qualified to advise Charles that all brides to be get nervous ahead of their weddings?' Matthew asked as Collins steered the coach carefully through the busy traffic heading in both directions along Aldersgate Street, on the journey down to Stepney. 'Were you once betrothed yourself? Or perhaps married?'

'None of your business,' Adelaide replied as she gazed out of the window at the shops and street vendors' stalls that they were clopping past. 'But from what I've heard of marriage, they have every right to be nervous of it.'

'Marriage is a fine Christian institution,' Matthew insisted.

'Precisely,' Adelaide replied, 'but who wants to live in an institution?'

'I remember you,' Margery Enderby confirmed with a wan smile at Adelaide as she led them both into the kitchen of the humble cottage that went with the curacy of St Dunstan's. 'You were with the police the day that...'

'The day that your husband died, that's right,' Adelaide confirmed gently, in the hope that her reappearance at the cottage wouldn't stir up too many bad memories. 'I'm not with the police, but my father was here in his capacity as a doctor and I assist him in his practice.'

'Very nice, I'm sure,' Margery replied politely as she switched her gaze to Matthew, screwing her still reddened eyes as she searched her memory. 'Your face is familiar as well, young man, but I can't quite place it.'

Matthew smiled reassuringly. 'Hopefully a happier memory,' he said softly. 'I visited your husband a few weeks before his unfortunate demise, regarding two former soldiers to whom he'd been a padre in his younger days.'

'I remember now!' Margery exclaimed. 'You're a church minister, aren't you, and you explained that your clerical collar was at the laundry or something and I told you to get your wife to soak them in a mixture of vinegar and water. You told me that you weren't married and I remember thinking that this was a shame because — well anyway, you've obviously remedied that. This lady is your wife?'

'No,' Adelaide replied, rather too hastily for Matthew's liking.

Margery looked puzzled. 'Then why are you both here? And since you are, would you like a cup of tea? I have another visitor in the second room through there and I was about to boil the water. There's shortbread too, this morning. Mrs Mulholland — she's the vicar's wife — sent him over with it. Everyone's been *so* kind since Tom — well, since — you know?' Her face crumpled in grief and she sat down heavily at the table, her shoulders shaking as she hastily extracted what looked like a well soaked handkerchief from the sleeve of her tunic and pressed it to her face to muffle the sobs.

Adelaide looked into her lined face with sympathy and gestured with her eyes for Matthew to do or say something. He took the seat across from the grieving widow, took one of her hands in his and smiled.

'It's at times like this that we must trust in God's mercy. Just offer your grief to Him and He will share it with you and send down His love to bring you peace of mind.'

'I rather think that's a line best left to me, young man,' came an authoritative voice from the doorway to the adjoining room and both Adelaide and Matthew looked up in surprise at the tall grey-haired man with the Patrician face who was looking down at Matthew from his considerable height with a quizzical expression.

'I was merely offering Mrs Enderby comfort in her time of grief,' Matthew explained with a suggestion of irritation in his voice.

The man said, 'So I heard. Are you a clergyman, or a well-meaning imposter?'

'No-one could be so wicked as to pose as a man of God,' Matthew protested. 'My name is Matthew West and I'm from the East End Mission in Shadwell.'

'That Wesleyan lot?' the man asked, and Matthew realised for the first time that he was being interrogated by a man wearing a dog collar.

'You must be the vicar,' he stated rather than asked. 'The man who brought shortbread to go with his condolences.'

The man appeared to frown at this levity, then his face broke into a smile. 'Tea and sympathy are part of the Anglican creed. Yes, I'm Joseph Mulholland, Vicar of St Dunstan's. But I have the advantage over you, since I recognised your name just then. You're the street preacher that my parishioners are always telling me about. The man who's always on the street corner in Wapping on Saturday market days, seeking to convey the word of God in what must be the most difficult of circumstances.'

'He came to talk to Tom a few weeks before…' Margery began to explain before the tears overcame her again and this time it was Adelaide who sat down and took her hand in a gesture of sympathetic support.

'Your wife?' Mulholland asked.

Matthew shook his head. 'My companion is Adelaide Carlyle, daughter of one of the surgeons at the London Hospital and a candidate for the upcoming LCC elections. We came to visit Mrs Enderby in the hope that she could assist us in a matter which we're investigating.'

'Shouldn't that sort of thing be left to the police?' Mulholland asked suspiciously.

Adelaide offered to assist Mrs Enderby make some tea that they could all partake of in the next room. The two men took the hint and retired to the cramped little sitting room, where Matthew felt obliged to justify himself and confide in the vicar who was no doubt doing his best to assist the widow through some difficult days.

'We believe that the heart attack suffered by Mr Enderby may have been induced by poison,' he told Mulholland in little more than a whisper. 'And we also believe that the poison may have been administered by a lady who visited him shortly beforehand. We have reason to believe that Mrs Enderby can identify that lady from a photograph which Adelaide — Miss Carlyle — has in her bag. I'm sorry if we blundered in at a bad time.'

'There's never a good time for those in the throes of grief for the loss of a loved one,' Mulholland reminded him. 'As you should know, given what I'm assured is your outstanding work among the poor and needy.'

'I fear that some of my "poor and needy" are prone to exaggeration,' Matthew replied modestly. 'They are so downtrodden and generally beaten by the circumstances in which they find themselves that any hand held out in friendship is apt to be over-valued. But by reminding them that I do my work out of love for God, whose inspiration fuels my love for them, I'm able to bring a little comfort into their miserable lives.'

Mulholland smiled. 'Beautifully put, but with a modesty that does you credit. A modesty that goes so far as to persuade you not to hide behind the dog collar that we all wear to set ourselves apart from others with a vanity that I find uncomfortable.'

'It's not false modesty, I'm afraid,' Matthew said. 'Although ordained into the Wesleyan ministry I'm not entitled to wear the collar of office until I'm awarded my own living.'

'You have no church of your own?' Mulholland asked in genuine surprise.

Matthew shook his head. 'Not as yet, but ordinarily it causes me no concern, since it allows me better to emulate the actions of my great inspiration John Wesley. In fact, it's only been recently that my lack of a church of my own has proved to be an inconvenience.'

'My brother is due to marry shortly and I would dearly love to conduct the service but has nowhere in which to do so. Because Charles — that's the younger brother in question — is not a regular attendee at the local parish church in Clerkenwell, where we live, and his fiancée is similarly deficient in respect of her home parish of Farringdon, they have been unable to find an Anglican church in which to get married, or a minister prepared to conduct the ceremony. That being the case, then of course they cannot even publish the banns.'

Mulholland sighed. 'I am well aware of the stuffy intransigence of my Church in matters such as this, which is why I conduct so many services under common licence for those who wish to be married in this magnificent church to which it has been my privilege to have been called, but who do not have the residency qualifications. Perhaps I can be of service?'

'You mean that you'll conduct the service yourself, here in St Dunstan's?' he asked breathlessly.

Mulholland nodded. 'Yes and no. It wouldn't be the first time I've done this sort of thing, as I already mentioned and the Bishop of London is quite used to signing off on common licences for me. All we'll need is the date.'

'Of course,' Matthew enthused, 'and I'll get it to you within the next twenty-four hours, to make sure that you're not otherwise engaged on that day.'

'You forgot that part of my answer just then was a "no",' Mulholland said. 'I said that you may use this church and that I'll prevail upon the Bishop for the common licence. But I understood that *you* were to conduct the service.'

'But I can't,' Matthew protested.

Mulholland's eyes narrowed. 'You *are* ordained, or so you led me to believe.'

'Yes, of course,' Matthew confirmed, 'and I've conducted more than one marriage service under common licence down at the Mission. But St Dunstan's? I mean — it's — well, it's not a Wesleyan chapel.'

'It's a Protestant house of God, Matthew,' Mulholland said. 'You were raised in the Anglican tradition?'

'Of course — everyone was in those days.'

'That was only thirty years or so ago, by my estimate,' the vicar replied with a smile.

Matthew replied, 'Twenty-eight, if you're enquiring as to my age.'

'So how did you become drawn into the Wesleyan tradition?' Mulholland asked.

'It wasn't difficult. With the greatest respect to you, the pure Anglican form of worship is seen as somewhat exclusive for the ordinary men and women for whom it exists. I was therefore drawn to the books I read about the Wesley brothers and how they had come to the same realisation and taken the word of God out to the common folk in market places, on the docksides and in what the poet Blake called "dark Satanic mills". I was drawn to follow their example.'

While helping to arrange the tea things, Adelaide was steering the conversation carefully around to the main reason for her visit. The photograph of Mary Miller was hidden inside her bag and she was listening attentively to Margery Enderby's reminiscences about her late husband's work around the parish and her own interest in maintaining the soup kitchen in the spacious and beautiful church gardens that were visible through the kitchen window.

Adelaide realised that she would have to be the soul of tact when seeking confirmation of Mary Miller as the person who had visited Thomas Enderby on the day he died. The last thing she wanted to do was reveal to the still distraught widow that the almost saintly man whose actions were being recounted in detail had been murdered by someone he had taken into his study in the belief that she could assist in the spiritual education of the children of the parish. But she had planned what she was going to say and was awaiting a suitable prompt from Margery.

'And of course, he was always open to fresh ideas,' Margery said at last. 'Even on the day he died he was discussing with a lady who presented herself here the possibility of expanding the Bible School that was one of his pet schemes. He even offered her sherry.'

'On the subject of that lady,' Adelaide intervened in the softest voice she could summon up, which trembled somewhat as a result, 'the police have been searching for a woman who's been going round the local churches posing as a charity worker when she's nothing of the sort. She's harmless, seemingly, but the apprehension is that she might be sizing up those churches with a view to burglaries being conducted by others. Do you remember what that woman who visited your late husband looked like?'

Margery thought for a moment, then insisted, 'I'm sure it couldn't have been that lady, dear. She was very well spoken and well dressed. And Tom wasn't the sort to fall for confidence tricksters. Of course, he didn't live for long enough to tell me what he thought about that lady. What was her name now? "Mary" something or other. She was quite tall, with fairish hair and probably only in her early thirties, I would have said.'

It was now or never and Adelaide slipped the photograph from her bag and laid it on the kitchen table. 'Was this by any chance her?' she asked.

Margery's eyes flew wide open. 'Yes, that's her! You mean that in his very last consultation in his life's work, poor old Tom was being hoodwinked by a confidence trickster? That's awful! He was always so eager to promote the work of the parish, God bless him! He even came back out to the kitchen here during her visit, to ask if we might invite her to stay to dinner with us. The poor deluded lamb!'

The tears began to slide down her face as it crumpled and Adelaide reached out and took her hand consolingly. 'I'm *so* sorry to have brought you more pain, my dear. Perhaps my friend Matthew can bring you some more words of consolation. Or perhaps your vicar. You compose yourself while I carry these tea things through to them.'

'You've obviously made a study of John Wesley,' Joseph Mulholland told Matthew, 'so you'll be aware that, like you, he was brought up as an Anglican.'

'Indeed,' Matthew confirmed. 'His father was an Anglican vicar somewhere in Lincolnshire, as I recall.'

While he was speaking, Adelaide stopped outside the door, sensing they were still engaged in a private conversation.

'There are some of us who prefer to pursue what is rapidly becoming known as an "Evangelical" approach to our work,' Mulholland said.

Matthew turned to look at him in curiosity. 'I have heard my own work described as "evangelical" by those of the High Church who turn their noses up at God's work preaching among the less privileged.'

'So you would conclude that our approaches to our ministries are not too far apart?'

'Obviously not,' Matthew agreed. 'The only difference between us is that you choose to minister to others dressed in rich vestments and with a fine roof over your head, whereas my church is the street and the market place and the only cover over my head is that of a Mission building with a roof that leaks when it rains heavily.'

There was another moment's pregnant silence before Mulholland asked quietly, 'How would you like to perform God's work here in this church, Matthew? Not just for your brother's wedding, but on a permanent basis?'

Matthew turned, open-mouthed. 'Did I just mishear you?'

'I think not. Obviously we have need of a new curate here at St Dunstan's and you are ordained. As I understand it, your ordination would have been in the Anglican form and I imagine that you have enough post-ordination years to make your transfer to here acceptable to the Bishop. The same Bishop who will be granting the common licence for your brother's wedding and who normally follows the promptings of his vicars in the matter of the appointment of curates.'

'But why me?' Matthew asked, still utterly stunned by the offer and trying to come to terms with the changes that this would mean to his life. A permanent living. A reasonable income. A house free of charge. But, against that, the loss of the freedom to preach on the streets and in the market places.

'Why you?' Mulholland echoed. 'For the reasons we have just been discussing. Tom Enderby was a fine curate and had begun a form of "outreach" here that was showing promise. For too long the Anglican Church has regarded itself as somehow one level up from the streets and the people in it and Tom had begun a movement back towards evangelism. I wish to continue that process and preferably to accelerate it.'

'I'd obviously need time to consider it,' Matthew hedged, hoping that God would give him a sign and would preferably give it some priority in his busy schedule.

'While you're doing so, let me advise you that the living currently brings with it an annual stipend of some five hundred and fifty pounds and that we have in mind building a new rectory inside the church grounds. The old cottage that

Margery Enderby still occupies will be allowed to her rent free for the rest of her days in recognition of the fine work of her late husband and indeed of the pioneering work she did by his side. Which raises an important, if somewhat delicate, matter that I need to enquire into. You are unmarried?'

'Yes.'

'You have plans to marry? Or do you at least have a lady-friend? That delightful young woman we left consoling Margery Enderby in her kitchen, perhaps?'

'I dearly wish that were the case,' Matthew replied sadly. 'She's the daughter of a leading surgeon at the London Hospital and well above my league. What makes matters worse is that her childhood experiences of her own church left her with a disdain for religion generally and she would be the least likely woman I know to agree to become the wife of a lowly curate. And yet I love her dearly. One of the great crosses I bear is holding that love deep inside me, unable to declare it, for if I did she would laugh in my face and dismiss me from the one thing that currently binds us, which is her ambition to become a member of the London County Council, in which I am giving her such assistance as I can.'

'A sad burden indeed to bear,' Mulholland commiserated. 'But it's important to the work of any curate — and particularly the curate that we urgently require here at St Dunstan's — that he be married to a woman who can stand by his side and reach out to the parish the way that Margery Enderby did for several years.'

'I can hardly ask Miss Carlyle to marry me in order that I could take up your very tempting offer,' Matthew pointed out. 'And if I were ever to pluck up the courage to offer my hand to her, it would be motivated by the love and respect that I have for her and not in order to improve my professional standing in my own life's work. It threatens to break my heart, for beneath the stern and forbidding face that she displays to the rest of the world I sense a deep passion and commitment to whatever takes her heart. It would take a miracle, but were I married to her I would consider that I had already died and gone to Heaven.'

'You must obviously bear that burden alone, Matthew,' Mulholland said quietly, 'but I shall offer prayers that it be lifted from your shoulders. In the meantime, please give my offer serious consideration. We could consider appointing you even though you remain unmarried, but we would obviously encourage you to seek a wife.'

'If only God would grant my prayer, I would need no further encouragement,' Matthew replied, close to tears. 'There is only one woman I would choose for my wife and only God knows how much I need her. But your prayers would be most humbly appreciated.'

'It's the least I can do,' Mulholland replied, 'because in the same way that you need this woman, St Dunstan's needs a new curate.'

'And the former curate's widow is in need of your comfort,' came a quiet but authoritative voice from behind them and both men turned in surprise to see Adelaide walking through the door.

Mulholland rose quickly and covered his confusion with a swift response. 'I'll go to her immediately,' he offered, leaving Matthew red-faced, staring at Adelaide as the pit of his stomach threatened to reach his throat.

'How much of that did you hear?' he croaked.

'Enough,' Adelaide replied. 'Particularly the bit about praying for a miracle. But I believe that one makes one's own miracles and I just did. Not only did Margery Enderby recognise Mary

Miller as the lady who visited her late husband just before he allegedly suffered a heart attack, but she also recalled that he left his study briefly to consult her, thereby giving Mary enough time to slip the digitalis into his sherry.'

'So we've definitely got her?' Matthew asked, glad that Adelaide wasn't going to blast him where he stood for his temerity in discussing his ambition to marry her with a virtual stranger.

Adelaide smiled. 'We? You mean me, surely? Although admittedly you played your part.'

22

'Inspector Jennings was looking for you, urgently,' Carlyle told Matthew as he followed Adelaide into the mortuary. 'And what's led to that huge grin that you're both wearing?'

'Actually, Father, we have one each,' Adelaide joked, 'since it's obviously unhygienic to share a grin.'

'It must be good,' Carlyle said, 'for you to descend into anything as light-hearted as humour, so what do you have to tell me? One or the other of you, since both together would be too much to hope.'

'Mrs Enderby not only recognised the photograph of Mary Miller,' Adelaide gushed, 'but she also told me that there was a brief moment in which her late husband left his study while Mary Miller was in there alone, so she had time to add the digitalis to the sherry.'

'And I've been offered a promotion which I'm seriously thinking of taking,' Matthew added.

Carlyle shook his hand without asking what it was, then reminded him that Jennings wanted to see him.

'I'll be back tomorrow, to discuss the next public address before the election,' Matthew said to Adelaide.

Adelaide sat down heavily on one of the stools alongside the work bench and looked hard into her father's face. 'I know I like to pretend to be so adult and independent, Father, but if ever a girl needed her father's advice it's me, right now.'

Carlyle took her hand, felt her pulse and said, 'Your heart's racing, sweetheart. Take a few deep breaths while I make some tea.'

Five minutes later, as they sat side by side drinking tea, Carlyle asked, 'So what has Matthew done or said?'

'How did you guess it was Matthew?'

'Your pulse rate. Very few things could account for a reading that high, but in a mature woman who hadn't just finished a course of violent exercise it could only be an affair of the heart.'

Adelaide took a deep breath and her father made a professional note of the wavering tone in it that denoted deep emotional stress. 'Well, while we were down there, the vicar of St Dunstan's offered him the job vacated by poor old Tom Enderby's death. Then he mentioned that it really required a married man for the job. They didn't know that I was listening in — quite unintentionally, of course.'

'And?' Carlyle asked, almost as anxious as she seemed to be.

'And he told the vicar how much he loved me and how there was no-one else in his life and that he'd regard it as a Heaven-sent miracle if we were to be married.'

'And what was your reaction?'

'I nearly passed out with sheer pleasure!'

'Excellent!' Carlyle all but shouted. 'So have you accepted?'

Adelaide's face fell as she shook her head. 'That's just the point. When he realised later that I'd overheard and more or less asked me what my reaction was, I went all stupid and instead of asking him if he meant it I kind of pushed him away again. I think I may have missed my chance!'

Without further warning she burst into floods of tears and jumped off her stool to throw herself into her father's arms and sob inconsolably.

Carlyle held her tightly and whispered words of comfort and reassurance in her ear until she'd sufficiently calmed down, then invited her to resume her seat and drink some more tea before answering some questions.

'You'd like to be Matthew's wife, I take it?'

'Of course! I've spent the past hour or so realising how *much* I want that, but I'm just too proud to say so. Something inside my head keeps warning me not to show my weakness to any man. Isn't it awful? How did I get like this, Father? Is it Mother living on in me, do you think?'

'What happened to that straight-laced crusader for women's rights? That Boudicca fighting off the Romans, or that Joan of Arc leading the French to victory against the English?'

'I know, isn't it awful?'

'No — it's wonderful!' Carlyle assured her as tears began forming in the corners of his own eyes. 'Could you live happily as the wife of a church minister?'

'If it's Matthew, then yes, of course. I don't care what he does for a living.'

'The next question is how you intend to get down off your soap box for long enough to tell Matthew that your answer's "yes".'

'He hasn't asked me yet, has he?' Adelaide countered.

'No and the poor boy probably never will, unless you find some way of making it clear to him that you won't wither him with a blast from your dragon mouth if he as much as hints at it.'

'Am I really that bad?'

'Sometimes. Particularly when you feel vulnerable.'

'Mary Miller's insisting that she won't speak to anyone else,' Jennings told Matthew, 'so you just got elected. She's down in the women's cells. We brought her here to the Yard, rather than have her violated, or even murdered, by the scum in

Newgate.'

'But we don't need a confession any more,' Matthew enthused. 'We've got evidence from her fingerprints that she was in the room with Enderby, we've got Mrs Enderby able to identify her as the woman left alone with the sherry while her husband left his study temporarily, and we can prove that a woman with her birth name visited Skuja at a time when they must have been planning his escape from the noose.'

'I'm an old-school bobby,' Jennings replied with a frown. 'We don't know how the fingerprint evidence might be accepted in court, eyewitness identification can always be challenged by smart-arsed lawyers, and her visits to Skuja can't be linked directly with the murder of Enderby, which is all that she's charged with at present. So a confession would go down very nicely just at this moment. Off you go — a turnkey will show you the way and you'll find their office near the ground floor entrance.'

The cell bars had a solid door in their centre and Mary Miller looked up with a wry smile as Matthew was admitted into the narrow space by a turnkey who told him that he'd be on the other side of the corridor door when required to let him out, which he could indicate by banging on the bars. Matthew thanked him, then turned back to look at Mary Miller, who was patting the space next to her on the bench.

'That ignoramus Jennings finally realised that there was only one person to whom I wished to unburden myself. Do come and sit beside me, handsome boy. I'm no longer as fragrant as I would have wished, but you're probably used to worse from your flock down in Shadwell. So what did you want to hear — my full confession?'

'That would be nice, but I'd certainly be intrigued to know how you managed to help your friend Skuja to dodge the noose.'

'He was no friend of mine,' Mary replied with a curled lip.

'So why did you organise his escape?' Matthew pressed her. 'It *was* you who visited him in Newgate several times before the day he was due to hang, wasn't it? Using your birth name of Bridget Dempsey?'

'He was a dirty rotten blackmailing bastard!' Mary insisted.

Matthew renewed his question. 'So why did you help him?'

'Why do you think? More blackmail.'

'But he was sentenced to death for setting fire to your late husband's chemist's shop and your husband had already committed suicide because of the deaths it caused, so what was there left to blackmail you about?'

'The money I'd been secreting away from the business behind my husband's back. The business was going bankrupt, certainly, but not because of declining trade — I was left in charge of the shop sales and half the money went into my purse rather than into the shop receipts.'

'So you were defrauding your own husband?'

'Why not? He wasn't any use to me in any other way and certainly not in bed. To be honest, he seemed to prefer young boys. So I took my satisfaction in other ways — with Artus Skuja, for one, once Andrew found him and arranged for the shop fire. That's how Skuja found out about the money I'd been putting aside and after he was sentenced to death and Andrew was dead, he got a message to me to visit him in Newgate. Then he threatened that if I didn't save him from the hangman he'll tell the insurance company about my secret hoard and I'd finish up penniless when they sued me for it. By then I'd set up my garment business and was threatened with ruin if Skuja carried out his threat.'

'So how was it done?' Matthew asked.

Mary smiled. 'Haven't you worked it out yet? Not even after all the trouble I went to showing you my underwear collection, some of which I was wearing at the time?'

'Never mind your underwear,' Matthew glowered, 'just tell me how you did it.'

'Too easy,' Mary said. 'The day before Skuja was due to hang, I came into the jail looking a bit fatter than usual, because I was wearing two corsets. My usual one, in addition to a special one for Skuja. It was fitted with an extra double row of bands with a loop in the top band, into which the two jailers fitted a hook. Then when the hangman was putting the noose over his head he also slipped a special extension to the rope into the hook. When the trapdoor opened, Skuja disappeared down the hole and was caught by the hook and left swinging. You all went for a cup of tea and it was a simple matter of the hangman going down to the lower level and cutting Skuja free. Then he was smuggled out of Newgate once it got dark.'

'Everyone attending that hanging — apart from the doctor, that is — must have been in on the plan,' Matthew concluded.

'Everyone except you, of course,' Mary said. 'John Tasker knew from previous hangings that you always looked away, or closed your eyes, so we made a point of requesting your attendance, to comply with the regulations. That was obviously our big mistake, because then John learned that you'd been investigating in the visitors' book, which is why I decided to approach you with a made up story about wanting to form a group to oppose the death penalty. Skuja was dead by then, of course, under his new assumed name of "Skelton".'

'You poisoned him?' Matthew queried, and when Mary nodded with a smile, he asked why that had been necessary.

'The bastard got too greedy. He wasn't happy that I was making such a success of my new garment business and demanded a cut of the profits in return for not peaching on me regarding the original matter of me defrauding my husband. I was making regular visits to his house, purely for sexual purposes, and we always had a glass of wine afterwards. It was easy to put something in his glass while I was pouring it the day before the rent was due, leaving his landlord to find the body.'

'Whose idea was it to kill off all the others who'd been a party to the faked hanging?'

'That was John Tasker again, once he found out that you were making enquiries. He was the one who lured Dr Somerskill out and knifed him in the back and the one who pushed the hangman under a bus. He also whacked Sam Tibbins over the head and shoved him into the river at Limehouse.'

'Even that hangman was a substitute, wasn't he?'

'Yes, after we gave the normal hangman a nasty dose of the squits with his evening meal. But we couldn't take the risk that anyone there that day would talk, and of course I had to eliminate that vicar from Stepney once we learned that you'd been to see him. We didn't know what you'd told him, you see.'

'You had me followed?'

'Every step for the past few weeks since you were unwise enough to go prying in that visitors' book.'

'But you didn't have me killed like all the others?'

'That was the original plan, and if it was left to Tasker you'd be dead already. But when I met you, I must admit that the lust that has ruined my life took over and I persuaded Tasker that it would be better to let me seduce you, then blackmail you into keeping quiet.'

'So am I still under threat from Tasker?'

'Who knows? He'll probably find some way of getting to me, even in here, when he finds out that I've been lumbered and wonders how much I've told you all about his involvement. He's a mean bastard, even when in a rare good mood, so if God really does look over you, then you'd both better keep a good look-out.'

'Any idea where Tasker is now?'

'None whatsoever. For all I know he's pulling the same trick with the spare rope and the corset in return for money and he certainly won't take kindly to any more interference from you. Best to keep your head well in.'

Matthew rose from the bench, thanked Mary for her candour and turned to leave. He banged on the cell bars to attract the attention of the turnkey, then just as he was about to leave the cell Mary called out to him.

'I don't know how you resisted my advances, but if it's not because you also prefer boys, then best hurry up and marry that doctor's daughter, before somebody else does.'

23

It always seemed to be windy whenever Matthew and Adelaide visited Spring Gardens, but today neither of them noticed as the excitement grew inside each of them. Adelaide was lined up with all the other hopeful candidates for the LCC elections and the vote counting had been completed. It was the culmination of weeks of campaigning on street corners, in public parks, and everywhere else where they had managed to attract a crowd of more than two. Adelaide couldn't have made her plans to turn London on its head any clearer to the voters and Matthew had almost run out of ways of introducing her. They'd both done their best and now, as Matthew stood in front of the platform on which all the hopeful candidates were standing he was wishing her 'good luck' with every smile he could summon to his nervous face every time she looked down at him for encouragement and tried to hold down the modest dinner that her father had insisted that she consume ahead of the results being announced.

The modest crowd fell ominously silent as the returning officer appeared on the platform behind the hopefuls, who parted down the middle to allow him to walk somewhat pompously to the front of the platform, armed with a massively long scroll of paper and a loud hailer. He put the device to his lips and his plummy voice travelled down the wind, bouncing back off the walls of the LCC Headquarters Building as everyone hung on his every word.

'I, Edward Mountjoy, returning officer for the elections to office within the London County Council and by virtue of the authority vested in me, declare that the following votes were

196

cast in the voting that was conducted on the twelfth day of May in this year of our Lord 1893.'

The announcement of the results had been organised on an alphabetical 'ward' basis, which meant that the results for the Hackney Ward would not be read out until a few more minutes had elapsed. Each minute seemed like an hour as Adelaide and Matthew exchanged nervous smiles while the results for the other wards were declared, then finally came the moment that they had worked towards for three months.

'For the Hackney Ward,' the returning officer declared. 'Graham Michael Edmunds, Progressive Party, nine hundred and forty two votes. Gerald Molyneux Mordaunt, Moderate Party, seven hundred and twelve votes. Adelaide Kathleen Carlyle, Independent, five hundred and sixty three votes. Peter John Grant, Independent, two hundred and three votes. I hereby declare Graham Michael Edmunds and Gerald Molyneux Mordaunt to be the duly elected councillors for the Hackney Ward.'

Adelaide maintained a poker face as the implications sank in. She was tempted to explode with frustration and accuse the successful male candidates who had deprived her of office of having bribed enough voters to ensure that yet again there would be no woman on the LCC. Then she caught the look of disappointment and defeat written all over Matthew's face and reminded herself that he had worked as hard as she had and, being Matthew, probably regarded her defeat as a personal failing on his part. Well, she could at least correct that mistake.

As the cheers of the successful supporters died down and the returning officer made his way back inside the building, the candidates left the platform to be either congratulated or consoled by those of their family and friends who had turned out to support them. Matthew was standing with Constance

Wilberforce on his right, as she maintained a verbal barrage of 'boo' every few seconds, interspersed with the occasional cry of 'shame', while Emily Peveril, to his left, was loudly demanding a recount, or an appeal. Only Matthew remained silent as Adelaide walked up to them with a stern countenance and an apology.

'I'm sorry you wasted so much of your time on a lost cause,' she told them.

Matthew was having none of that. 'You got over five hundred votes,' he reminded her. 'That's five hundred and more people who believed that the LCC should have a woman member. And you didn't come last.'

'I may as well have done,' she replied gloomily, 'for all the long-term effect I've had. At least I can devote my time to working with my father and learning more about medicine, instead of wasting it addressing the blind regarding the inequalities in our society so far as it treats women. And what will you do with your free time, Matthew?'

He hesitated for a moment, then decided that she was entitled to be the third person to know. 'I've accepted that curacy in Stepney.'

'I thought that it required a married man.'

'Yes, it does,' he admitted, red-faced. 'I'll have to get to work on that now that I have more free time available to me.'

A week later, after Matthew had successfully conducted the marriage of Charles and Susan West, he waved goodbye to Joseph Mulholland on the vicarage doorstep and made his way down the long winding downhill path through the churchyard and into the High Street, where he could catch a late bus that would take him into Whitechapel for the connecting service north into Clerkenwell. Until the new curate's house was completed he was still residing with his parents, rather than inconvenience either the Mulhollands or Margery Enderby, but he spent his days at St Dunstan's, learning what he could of his future duties, getting to know his new parishioners and taking pleasant meals with his mentor the vicar.

The superintendent of the East End Mission had wished him all the best in his new-found role, but Matthew was still experiencing guilt pangs at having selfishly accepted this new career opening, and his thoughts were engaged on how he might find some means to bring the Mission within the overall purview of his new ministry when a figure stepped out in front of him in the shadow between two street lamps. He stopped momentarily, then froze when the figure stepped into the pool of light just in front of him and he recognised the rotund double-chinned face of John Tasker wearing an evil grin.

'Evenin' yer Reverence,' Tasker sneered. 'Hope yer kept up yer membership wi' God, 'cos yer about ter need ter show yer membership card.'

'Meaning what, precisely?' Matthew asked challengingly, hoping that the quiver in his voice didn't sound as loud to Tasker as it did to him.

'What d'yer fink? It's your turn now. I done fer all the rest, an' now it's just you what's left. Serves yer right fer nosin' about in that visitors' book.'

'You and who else?' Matthew challenged him.

Tasker grinned as he nodded past Matthew's shoulder. He turned quickly and two brawny looking men were creeping up on him. Matthew stepped further out into the roadway, turning side on to the assailants on both sides of him, then felt a massive blow to the back of his head as he was struck from behind and everything went black.

'Right!' Tasker commanded his three accomplices, 'Grab a hold've 'im and take 'im down ter the river. Then we chuck 'im in, like we did the last 'un.'

They were about to lift Matthew from the roadway when there came a shout, the sound of a whistle and the noise of pounding footsteps, and the group scattered in different directions, leaving Matthew lying in the roadway, seemingly dead to the world.

24

'For the third time,' Carlyle told Adelaide testily from the far side of the hospital bed in which Matthew was lying comatose, 'he's not going to die. His pulse is steady and to judge by the soundings I'm getting from his heart he's capable of pulling five railway carriages uphill.'

'But he's not showing any signs of life!' Adelaide all but wailed.

Her father tutted. 'That's because he's unconscious. This doesn't mean that he's about to expire, trust me, because as you may have noticed he's still breathing normally. In due course he'll come to, but for a while he may be a bit groggy and talking nonsense.'

'Then I'll know he's back to normal,' Adelaide joked feebly as she fought back the tears. 'And if you can keep him alive, I'll be grateful to you for the rest of my life.'

'You should save your gratitude for Inspector Jennings, who had the energy and intelligence to resume the search for Tasker, as the result of what Mary Miller told Matthew and after one of Jennings's men got that tip-off. And of course you must thank whoever supplied that tip-off, who I suspect was someone else who felt threatened by Tasker, although I don't recall anyone else being involved in Skuja's subterfuge. Matthew was the last on his list, so far as I know.'

'How long do you think it'll be before Matthew regains consciousness?' Adelaide asked nervously.

'You can never tell with these things. An hour, maybe more. Perhaps not even until tomorrow, who knows? There's a certain amount of eyelid flutter, which suggests that he may be coming to, so perhaps you'd better stay where you are.'

'I wasn't thinking of just walking away from the man I love while he's lying there so vulnerable. I just want him to wake up so that I can tell him how much I love him.'

'Can I get that in writing?' came a hoarse whisper from the bed, and Carlyle and Adelaide looked down in amazement at Matthew's open eyes and stupid grin.

'Whatever you thought you heard just then was the result of your blow to the head,' Adelaide said stiffly.

Matthew chuckled. 'If it was a dream, can I go back to it, please? And why is my head pounding like this, anyway?'

'You got a massive whack on the back of it,' Carlyle told him. 'You're lucky that your skull's so thick, so there's unlikely to be any permanent damage. But you may find that your vision's a bit blurry for a while.'

'It's coming back to me now — Tasker!' Matthew shouted as he attempted to sit upright, then fell back with a cry of pain. 'My head hurts!'

'As it has every right to do,' Carlyle told him. 'And if you try to get up again I won't be responsible for the consequences. Don't worry about Tasker — Jennings has him safely locked away in his own jail. Apparently the governor of Newgate was most put out when he found himself admitting one of his most trusted men and was advised that he was responsible for Skuja escaping from under his nose.'

'So that's everything completed then,' Matthew sighed contentedly.

'Hardly,' Adelaide corrected him.

'What's left?' Matthew asked.

'You have to secure your new position in St Dunstan's by finding a wife, if you recall. Or has the blow to the head driven that completely out of your mind?'

'I've found someone who I want to marry,' Matthew said.

There was a long silence, broken when Adelaide's patience failed her and she asked, 'Well?'

'Well what?'

'Well who's the lucky lady?'

'I can't tell you because I haven't asked her yet and she might turn me down.'

'When do you intend to ask her?'

'When I'm back on my feet and can kneel properly at *her* feet in the approved manner when I ask for her hand.'

'And what makes you think she might turn you down?'

'I'm only a humble curate and she's a fine lady with a wealthy father.'

'Who is she?'

'Take a guess.'

'Oh for Heaven's sake!' Carlyle muttered as he took hold of Matthew's hand and asked him to look him in the eyes. Believing it to be some sort of medical procedure, Matthew complied and Carlyle asked, 'Do you wish to marry my daughter? Answer me immediately, or I'll get Sister to administer an enema!'

'Yes, I do,' Matthew grinned back stupidly.

Carlyle sighed with satisfaction. 'Step One complete. Step Two is to ask for my permission.'

'May I please marry your daughter?'

'You may — if she consents.'

It fell silent for a moment, until Carlyle turned to smile across the bed at Adelaide. 'You heard that?'

'Yes,' Adelaide replied in a liquid voice that denoted impending tears.

Carlyle turned back to Matthew. 'As you just heard, my daughter was witness to your expressed desire to marry her and she hasn't exploded in rage, or told you to go and take a running jump. Now, what have you to say to her?'

'Thank you for not being angry,' Matthew said mischievously.

Adelaide tutted with frustration. 'Don't you have something to ask me?' she demanded.

'Yes. What would be your reaction if I were to ask you to become the wife of the Curate of St Dunstan's?'

'That would depend on who he was.'

'And if it were me?'

'Then I'd say yes.'

'Well go ahead, then.

'Go ahead and do what?'

'Ask me.'

Adelaide looked helplessly across at her father, who was grinning broadly as he nodded. 'You heard me give my consent,' he reminded her.

Adelaide leaned forward and took Matthew's other hand as she asked, 'Matthew West, may I become the wife of the Curate of St Dunstan's? If you tell me no, I'll get one of those bedpans from the pile in the corner and batter your head in.'

'Hardly the most romantic proposal a man ever received, but the answer's yes and I've won,' Matthew grinned broadly.

'You've won my hand, obviously, but what do you mean?' Adelaide demanded.

Matthew chuckled. 'What I mean is that Madame Ice Face, the terror of all men everywhere, has finally descended from her soap box and asked a man to marry her.'

Carlyle burst into peals of spontaneous laughter that obliged the Sister seated at the end of the ward to call for silence. As it descended, Adelaide was recovering her wits.

'There are of course conditions,' she insisted. 'For a start I don't intend to spend the rest of my life boiling your dog collars. I want to continue to work with Father in the mortuary.'

'Agreed. I have one, too.'

'What's that?'

'That you have another try at the LCC.'

'Gladly,' Adelaide grinned.

'So it looks as if we have an agreement that requires only the seal of God. I'm sure the vicar will agree to do the honours.'

'Thank God!' Carlyle muttered. 'I no longer have to watch the pair of you walking warily round each other like a couple of prize fighters.'

'I should have shown my feelings sooner,' Adelaide said as she leaned down and kissed Matthew firmly on the lips. 'I think I've loved you since that very first day when you all but battered down to the door to our basement laboratory.'

'For me it was when you held my hand and poured neat iodine into the cuts on my face.'

'From such things is true love made,' Carlyle said happily. 'Mind you, I think you may have established a new tradition between you. Marriages are meant to be made in Heaven, but yours appears to have been made in a mortuary.'

A NOTE TO THE READER

Dear Reader,

Thank you for taking the time to read this second novel in my 'Carlyle and West' series. I hope that you were inspired to do so by having read the first in the series and that you will go on to read the rest. As usual I was able to weave much actual historical fact into the narrative.

First of all, the emerging police practice of fingerprinting. It was as described in the pages you have just read, since after the Frenchman Alphonse Bertillon began his experiments to distinguish between people by means of their various bodily features, eugenicist Sir Francis Galton was approached by Charles Darwin with the idea that each individual might be found to possess their own unique fingerprints, a theory that went back as far as the Ancient Babylonians. The Metropolitan Police began to collect finger impressions in the 1890s and it is not therefore stretching things too far to suggest that they enlisted the help of surgeons such as James Carlyle. However, it would be 1902 before fingerprints were first offered as evidence in English criminal courts.

Likewise the harrowing process of public hanging, with its grisly rituals in which our hero Matthew West finds himself involved as the attending clergyman required by Government regulation. By the 1890s England was making use of the relatively humane 'long drop' method, which calculated the 'optimum' drop by reference to the condemned man's body weight. Too short a drop and the victim would suffer death by slow strangulation, while too long a drop all but guaranteed a decapitation. Little wonder that we look back on the death penalty with such horror. The public hangman identified in this novel as James Billington really existed and was the 'first choice' public hangman during the period covered by this novel.

Then there was the matter of male dominance of the London County Council, formed in 1889 following the scandals that had plagued its predecessor the Metropolitan Board of Works. It had its first headquarters in Spring Gardens, in the West End splendour of St James's and it elected exclusively male councillors until an Act of Parliament in 1907 officially recognised the right of women to sit on County Councils. Prior to that, two women — Jane Cobden and Margaret Sandhurst — had been elected by popular vote, but had been silenced by successful legal challenges to their right to take part in LCC business.

This suppression of female emancipation was of course the principal reason for the emergence of organisations such as the Women's Franchise League and pressure groups such as the 'Suffragists' and 'Suffragettes' dedicated to more direct action — much of it unlawful — that would not see their demands met until after Britain had survived the Great War, when women earned their spurs in activities such as munitions work. At the same time their more demure, and certainly more law-abiding, sisters were knocking angrily on the door of professions such as medicine and the law and Adelaide Carlyle is faithfully portrayed, with affection, as a lady of her times.

I was on less confident ground regarding Matthew's return to the Anglican fold after a successful and dedicated period following in the footsteps of his hero John Wesley. All that was written about Wesley and the Methodist movement was historically accurate; he was indeed the son of an Anglican vicar from Lincolnshire and he was ordained in the Church of

England before he and his brother Charles were called to minister to the poor and downtrodden for whom Anglican churches were almost forbidden places.

Methodism, and its more austere predecessor the Wesleyan movement, remained staunchly Anglican in nature and commitment and even after the formation of the Wesleyan Methodist Church in England converted into an institution what had been launched as a form of evangelical Anglicanism the only real distinction between the two church movements was really one of social class and liturgy. It is highly feasible that Matthew West might be tempted back into the 'mother Church' in the circumstances in which he found himself, and I have only engaged in what may have been artistic licence in the matter of his re-ordination.

I hope that you enjoyed this second novel in the series and that you are eager to follow the subsequent history of Matthew, James and Adelaide. The next novel in the series covers the period of their engagement in not only marriage preparations, but also the fight against recruitment of disaffected youth into criminal gangs in the late Victorian East End.

I would welcome any feedback and support that you, the reader, can supply. You can, of course, write a review on **Amazon** or **Goodreads** or you can contact me online via my Facebook page: **DavidFieldAuthor**. I'm more than happy to respond to observations, reviews, questions, or anything else that occurs to you, or to join in any 'thread' that you care to begin.

I look forward to getting to know you better online.

David

davidfieldauthor.com

Sapere Books is an exciting new publisher of brilliant fiction and popular history.

To find out more about our latest releases and our monthly bargain books visit our website:
saperebooks.com

Printed in Great Britain
by Amazon

78955657R00121